Absolutely Hutely

Dan and Hutely Discover the Ancient Ways of China

Dan Tilley

The Reading Glass Books
(888) 420-3050
www.readingglassbooks.com
production@readingglassbooks.com

Table of Contents

Music Soundtrack

Lyrics and music written and performed by Dan Tilley

1. When Love Leaves

2. Cities of the Shang

3. Patterns

4. Play in the Sand

5. Everyday Life

6. Got to Know Everything

7. The Enlightened One

Cast of Characters

In order of appearance

Fu Sheng: historian, minor Zhou official, and philosopher.

Qin Shi Huang Di: (Zheng) first emperor of a unified China; Legalist.

Qin Li Si: Grand Counselor; Legalist enforcer.

Dan: modern college student; time traveler; discovers ancient ways of China.

Hutely: graduate of the Historical Guide Academy; guides Dan through ancient history.

Kwan Yin: Holy Mother of Compassion; guardian angel of humans.

Chang: Taoist goddess; time traveler; love interest of Fu Su.

Fu Su: son of Zheng turned Confucianist; time traveler.

Chu Yuan: magic ferry operator; started Dragon Boat Festival; patriotic icon.

Jade Dragon: sent by Jade Emperor to protect Confucian Classics.

Tu Ti: God of the earth; represents God of Five Roads.

Song: (King Cheng) child king; early Zhou Dynasty.

Duke of Zhou: wrote Book of Changes; inspired other Confucian Classics.

Fenhua: descendant of royal concubines; graduate of Confucian School.

Jia Yi: resurrected Chu Yuan's nine-poem lament.

Madame Sheng: Fu Sheng's daughter; book translator for Han Dynasty.

Introduction

Suddenly there comes a realization in an isolated region of the world. The inhabitants were given a chance to progress unhindered from the intrusion of outside forces. A profound self-awareness arose among this early river civilization. Like timeless divine messages that span the centuries for thousands of years, early river civilizations evolved and flourished on several continents. This was especially true on the Asian continent.

Time is and has always been on China's side. The Portuguese say they discovered China in 1506, or was it 1503? No matter. To the contrary, China was already thousands of years old. You could say that self-discovery was a way of life on the Yellow River. An old Taoist priest asked a visiting American in the late nineteen thirties if he had chosen a side in the upcoming world conflict. The priest lived on a remote mountaintop in west China, but somehow, he understood the global issues of the day. His culture's willingness to educate each other led to his awareness.

First off, ancient Chinese literature gave them "The Five Civilizing Books" that are better known as the "Confucian Classics." In these books, personality is defined by actions as they relate to society but not individual actions. These books are filled with songs, documents, life changes, seasonal annals, and ancient rites. A major theme, or discourse, that plays out through Chinese history that exemplifies this awareness is Cultural Homogeneity. It is a social uniformity concept that includes five sub-topics, and they are as follows: muscle-power technology, concubines that led to depressed descendants of the nobility, traveling storytellers and informative puppet shows, a country-wide examination system, and filial piety. The latter includes five designated relationships that tell the poorest of the poor up to the emperor how to behave.

Related to filial piety, ancestor worship has been at the spiritual core of Chinese society. Through the years, the "God of Five Roads" has bridged the gap between the living and the dead. It is a positive worship that influences behavior.

These meaningfully reciprocal experiences and purposeful themes would have strengthened common bonds or elasticity in any society, unless antagonistic, powerful forces plotted to silence the chords of social correspondence.

Confucianism is just one Chinese school of thought touched on in the book. There are five altogether. Each one winds its path through Chinese history within the ceremony of the people and ruling elite. They are Confucianism, Taoism, Legalism, Buddhism, and most recently, Communism. In the context of this book, Confucianism and Taoism function as protagonists trying to reestablish the enlightened reign of Zhou leaders like the Duke of Zhou and his nephew, Song. These rulers dedicated themselves to making society a better place even at the risk of personal peril. Conversely, Legalism acts as the antagonist to Confucianism and Taoism's common, caring influence throughout the ages. Other interpretations of both Confucianism and Taoism lean toward Legalist thought. Legalism's harsh conformity requirements led to hardship and deaths.

Confucius didn't consider himself an "Innovator"; rather, he was a spokesperson espousing timeless principles that Zhou sages put into practice in a romanticized past. Happiness could be achieved by following one's own principles (Li) through education and self-realized action. Confucianism and Taoism are cast in a positive light here, but one can't ignore the unifying impact that Legalism afforded the short-lived Qin Dynasty. One might conclude that Taoism played a part in this unification. China got its name from the Qin despite their cruel, extreme methods toward unification. Legalism often identified itself with Taoism because of its mystical, solitary commune with nature. Its lack of initial social activism gave little resistance to Legalistic domination, but eventually Legalism elicited Taoist rebellion. Confucianism and Taoism both claim to be the true "Way."

Taoism's principles are written in the TAO TE CHING. Lao Tsu is the Tao's best-known professor of this organic, natural concept.

Both Confucianism and Taoism may have their origins in the latter stages of the Zhou Dynasty. Unlike Confucianism, Taoism insists that less government is always a clever idea. Taoists sought to understand the natural world to find their "Way" in everyday life. They were the alchemists seeking a nature-based ordering of things rather than the constant political upheaval of man-made, structured society that attributed to Confucianism.

Taoist priests helped facilitate the Buddhist school of Chinese thought that originated in India. Both faiths have a subtle intellectualism. Taoists, as stated earlier, were mindful chemists of the elements, while Buddhism had specific guidelines to avoid suffering. The Eightfold Path and the Four Noble Truths were given to followers by the enlightened Siddhartha Gautama (Buddha). He sought to lessen the traumatic burden of human experience.

Finally, Communism arose out of the chaos of Europe during the Industrial Revolution. Karl Marx's words resonated with Mao Tse-Tung who established a communist state, the People's Republic of China. After foreign invasion, occupation, and failed policies caused the Chinese to experience suffering on a large scale, the Chinese countryside gained control over the industrializing cities in 1949. Chairman Mao ruled China after he staged a long, codifying march across the Chinese countryside. "Workers of the world unite" was a popular slogan in response to the inhumane practices of industrialization.

By the 1980s, economic reforms were instituted to counter the disastrous effects of Mao's "Cultural Revolution" and "Great Leap Forward." Persecution of intellectuals and absurd economic policy characterized post-revolution China. This process of political change and reform defines China's previous dynastic cycles as well. American capitalists bestowed China with a "Most Favored Nation" status with the West. It really started in the 1970s, and its consequences are inescapably felt today. We will focus our attention, however, on ancient China with just a few references to the present. In 2023 China has become a "Surveillance society." There is a return to Maoist dogma that epitomizes Xi Jinping's authoritarian leadership of over a billion Chinese citizens.

If experience is indeed the teacher, then China had a lot to say. Because of its early relative isolation, China was given plenty of time to say it. To the dismay of many, China has returned to Maoist principles exemplified by censorship of the press and individuals promoting human rights. It seems dogmatic ritual has replaced the once-prominent Confucian-inspired examination system. Confucianism and Taoism's heated, dynastic relationship was traditionally cooled by enlightened Buddhist intervention. Intrusive industrial, high-tech advances are replacing the old communal muscle-power technology.

In conclusion, the Confucian Classics may be orientated toward society as a whole, but the Confucian exams taught individual students to take the moral high ground in the pursuit of happiness for all. Furthermore, Confucianism, Taoism, and Buddhism sought to alleviate people's suffering through education. In sharp contrast, the Legalist school of thought sought only to accentuate the power of the emperor. The cruel tactics of unification by the Qin was an existential threat to the Concept of Homogeneity and ancient Chinese social correspondence.

As with most Americans, I'm rarely at a loss for words. But a long list of ancient Chinese innovations and good ideas gives me reason to pause and leaves me speechless. As I dozed off to sleep, I kept hearing a voice repeating the same phrase over and over. It said, "Fifth child, five roads, and five classics to save."

Chapter 1

. . . .

A Rude Awakening

It was indeed a rude awakening for Fu Sheng who had been a fierce opponent of Qin Shi Huang Di and Grand Counselor Li Si. They were the Qin tribal leaders. They defeated the seven tribes remaining in China after the "Warring States Period." Inflicting a brutal Legalist code of law, they set out to erase all vestiges of the Zhou Dynasty, especially the "Confucian Classics." Fu Sheng, a philosopher, historian, and minor Zhou official in his own right, sought out friends, scholars, and former Zhou officials to obtain copies of the classics to add to his scroll of documents. These officials had obtained magic paper from the future.

Scouring the countryside of Shandong province near Louyang, he met up with an old friend, Wang, who took Fu Sheng down to the Wei River. On the shore were six green, glowing book covers. Fu Sheng covered each copy of the classics with the protective covers. Historians began unraveling their scrolls and covering them with square covers in the hopes the Qin soldiers wouldn't recognize them. Fu Sheng did the same. He thanked Wang with heartfelt bows and tried to flee south to avoid the soldiers.

Unfortunately, he and his handcart full of books were captured and taken to Luoyang. He was now a prisoner of the Qin. To the dismay of the Zhou-educated elite, the soldiers were tipped off regarding scroll hiding. Soldiers built large fires and began burning anything square or rectangular and any scrolls they could find. Those with Legalist scrolls were pardoned and allowed to keep them. Cherished possessions also perished in the flames. Fortunately for Fu Sheng, he was small, and he could easily hide among the woman and children to avoid execution.

A rude awakening was putting it mildly as I hit the ground running in an ancient Chinese cultural center. I felt like I was in Nazi Germany or Stalinist Russia. There were huge bonfires and screams echoing from every direction. Soldiers were rounding up people, confiscating property, and burning belongings. I struggled to maintain my footing alongside the mass of people fleeing for their lives.

"Dan! Over here!" a familiar voice whinnied. "Get on quick!"

"Hutely, is that really you?"

"How many talking donkeys do you know, my boy?"

"You're the only one I know. So tell me, what the heck is happening, Hutely? I was taking five, and the next thing I know, I'm running with the bulls. I heard a voice talking about the fifth child, five roads, and five classics. Then suddenly, and without a complimentary warning, here I am."

"No time to explain, Danny boy. We must save the Millet Ruler's legacy and awaken the sacred oracle bones of the dragon."

"Now wait a cotton-picking millet; I mean minute."

"Must I always guide humans? They always seem like they just crawled out of bed," Hutely grunted as he flipped me onto his back.

"I did just get out of bed. In fact, I was hurled out of bed with little crawling. Okay, okay, there was some crawling," I said, wishing I were back in bed. At that moment, a huge crowd was gathering in the town center which Hutely referred to as Luoyang.

"Did you say dragon?" I asked, trying hard not to freak out.

"Don't worry, Dan. At least we're dealing with an animal on this one."

"Yeah, that's right!" I quivered then quickly added, "They fly, breathe fire, and eat humans, don't they? Aren't they reptiles?"

"Relax, Dan. Do you remember what the Fifth Dimension said?" Hutely asked in a nonchalant tone.

"Absolutely, Hutely, I remember. It went something like 'One last bell to answer and one less egg to fry'?"

"Nice try, Dan, but you've got it all wrong. They said, 'Let the sunshine, let the sunshine in. Then peace will guide the planets and love will steer the stars.' No doubt there are good and bad dragons throughout history. Speaking of fire, there's a burning ember heading straight for your head. Get down, Dan!"

Like an air defense system with hair that smells just as bad as it kicks, Hutely sprang into action. He reared up and high-hoofed the meteoric ember. Then he started filling me in on the mission the H. G. Academy volunteered us for.

"You see, Dan, the phrase in your dream refers to the important civilizing forces in ancient China. What we are witnessing are the remnants from the Shang Dynasty which melded into the Zhou Dynasty. The Zhou fell to the Qin Dynasty, to which China now owes its name. They wielded supreme power espousing Legalist doctrine."

"China is named after these murderers! That really gets under my skin."

"Funny you should say that."

"What's that supposed to mean?" I asked Hutely, feeling chills running up and down my spine. "All I can say is—" Before I could finish, and to our amazement, music started coming from one of the bonfires. Hutely and I listened carefully. Suddenly we realized we were in the song and the song was in us.

> *When love leaves, what takes its place?*
> *A young man asked seeing through old eyes.*
> *Nature's great healing fate, loving breath our only gate.*
> *Angels of mercy turn night to day.*
> *When love leaves, what takes its place?*
> *An old mule asked seeing through young eyes.*
> *Nature's weight, a golden state, forgotten loves take new shape.*
> *Angels of mercy then save the day.*
> *When love leaves, what takes its place?*
> *A nation asks awaiting the sunrise.*
> *Nature creates a new mandate, love never leaves the golden rays.*
> *Angels of mercy turn night to day"*

Not knowing what to do next, Hutely did what came naturally. But since he couldn't find anything to eat, he started his latest history lesson instead. The only difference was it was our present day.

"You see, Dan, most dynasties in China started out being benevolent. The ruling elite claim the 'Decree of Heaven.'"

"Oh really! Are the people here waiting for the right moment to toast marshmallows, chestnuts, and s'mores?"

"This one is different, and that is why we are here."

"Absolutely, Hutely. I'll start looking for good roasting sticks," I said sarcastically. "All right, all right, I know what you're saying. It's like Plato's philosopher king who was supposed to be cool and benevolent toward the people. But it never happened, and poor Plato was sold into slavery."

"Very good, Dan, the memories still reside in you. Hopefully, they reside in all of us. Well, at least love never leaves permanently. Remember the song?" Hutely shouted as the crowd noise grew while reacting to the arrests.

"What do you mean love never leaves permanently? Oh, right... the song!" I yelled as the book burning intensified.

"Love, she has arrived!" Hutely exclaimed excitedly.

"What in the world is this?" I gasped. Hutely and I looked to be overrun by beautiful angels, large animals, and babies. Hutely began to chainsaw an explanation.

Chapter 2

. . . .

The Holy Mother of Compassion

"She, my boy, is a holy mother of compassion. Her name is Kwan Yin." Hutely began telling me the story of the goddess Kwan Yin as her angels of mercy descended all around us. Kwan Yin was glowing and wearing flowing white robes and riding on a multicolored lotus flower. There was an incredible light that was shown through and around her. A yellow, red-lined halo rose like the sun behind her black hair and beautiful face. In a reverent, giddy-up voice, Hutely continued explaining. "She symbolizes protection and relief for those in need, Danny boy. She is considered the guardian angel of all humans and the patroness of mothers and sailors. She suffered a cruel father while in an imposed exile at a temple. Her father secretly arranged her fate."

Suddenly another goddess arrived on the scene. "It's nice to see you again, Hutely!" Chang yelled while giving me a so-so look. Chang had bright green eyes like the color of jade and jet-black hair which hugged her milky white skin. She wore a short gold silk dress and thatch sandals. Her slender body had the look of a gymnast. After giving Hutely a quick hug and a pet on his mane, she slowly walked my way. She kept a keen eye on Kwan Yin's forces and a skeptical eye on me. Nevertheless, she began to tell her story to me while Hutely shielded us from the conflagration.

"My mother, Chango, loved life to the fullest. Unfortunately, my father, Yi, shot suns out of the sky with his mighty bow and deadly arrows. The gods became angry. My family was stripped of our immortality. Fortunately, mother and I were given a potion for immortality by a sympathetic goddess. Mom and I drank our potions along with my dad's portion," Chang said sorrowfully.

"Well, where was he? Surely he isn't hunting any more suns," I added hesitantly.

"If he does, there will be only darkness. There is but one known sun now to warm the Earth. My mother, Chango, felt isolated, so she floated to the Moon. Yi remained a unique mortal, and he travels to see her one day out of the year. On the full Moon, they stay in a splendid palace made of cinnamon wood which he built for her."

"And now you are here in the center of the storm. Why? Pray tell?" I asked. Before she could answer, I added, "Talk about your dysfunctional family. Absence does make the heart grow fonder."

"I suppose, but I do miss them both dearly. And as you must know, Dan, my mother became an angel of the Moon. My father searches for new suns so he can atone for his actions. Wherever weapons are used to extinguish the light, you will find me. Kwan Yin took me to the H. G. Academy where I met Hutely. I now travel time when Hutely needs my help," Chang said glowingly. She seemed to lighten up when she mentioned the master mule.

"It's always a pleasure for us animals to help. I know you agree, Dan," Hutely grunted graciously.

"I'm not an animal, Hutely," I said.

"Ah, but you wish you were. Just think about all we've done for humans, Dan, and how my brethren helped Kwan Yin," Hutely belched out after vacuuming up a stranded rice bowl.

"This sounds like another up with animals' story, Hutely," I groaned as explosions rocked the square. Chang and I stayed close to Hutely as smoke filled our lungs and burned our eyes. Somehow, Hutely kept finding food scraps to eat while explaining his animals' comment.

"Up with animals? Now, now, Dan, hear me out. Animals living near the temple took pity on Kwan Yin, and they helped her with her tedious and time-consuming chores. Her wicked father imposed time-consuming burdens on her."

"Is there anyone you don't know, Hutely? And what's with all the men around here? One almost creates the ultimate nocturnal ice age, and another is mean to his extraordinary daughter who rescues babies. Not to mention the Qin whose favorite past times are terrorizing people and book burning, Jeez!"

"What do you mean by that, Dan?" Chang inquired with her deep jade-full eyes.

"Allow me to answer that, Chang," Hutely chuckled. "Jeez is short for Jesus, my lady. Like you might have said Confuz in China. That is short for Confucius, Dan."

"No-o-o," I said in a drawn-out voice. "You don't say, Hutely."

"Well, I do say this. The animals have arrived, and they're just in time," Hutely barked with pride.

"Oh yeah, and monkeys are going to fly out my... !" I added, wishing I hadn't. Suddenly, huge colorful, sparkling snakes began spouting water on the bonfires like viper firefighters. This allowed large orange, white, and black-striped tigers to separate five or six green glowing books from the burning wood. Kwan Yin and her maidens comforted the children whose parents had been killed by the Legalists. Victims had referred to the Legalists as murderers who thought only of empire and the absolute rule of the Qin emperor.

Heavenly birds brought the children fresh vegetables to purify their tormented souls. Kwan Yin didn't need water to douse the flames. A mere touch of her hand extinguished the hottest inferno. Chang and Kwan Yin embraced as if they were long-lost friends. Maybe Chang has an inferno needing to be extinguished, I thought as the drama unfolded. Hutely seemed to read my thoughts and gave me a swift kick on my set-down.

Many of the children were flown to Taoist temples (soon to have a Buddhist persuasion) for their protection by angels. Incredibly, the large pythons fought off the Qin warriors while the beautiful striped tigers carried the books to safety. The books were grand specimens; moreover, they were covered in what appeared to be alligator skin.

"Well, I'll be. Their mouths aren't burning, Hutely," I grimaced. Hutely's animal talk now had me fearing for the dental health of man-eating tigers. "Alligator book covers must be another Chinese invention."

"That's not alligator skin, Dan. That is Grade-A, prime cut, fire-breathing dragon skin. It doesn't get hot or burn. It protects the paper, but not the ink. However, the paper remembers if given the benefit of historical context. The ink will appear again if the books travel through time to the right dynastic periods. We were sent to ensure that the words (characters) in those books reappear. But we must remember, certain high-ranking Qin warriors don't wish us harm." Without warning and unfortunately for us, Hutely sneezed. It startled the fiercest Qin warriors with its booming rudeness.

"Way to go, Hutely," I said, gripping Chang's hand. "Just in case those killers didn't know where we were, they know now!"

Hutely turned to face me, grunted, and then wiped his snout on my sleeve. He was quick to add, "The Millet Ruler's existence was inscribed on bones. His legacy plays out through the many Chinese characters that tell of reforming times, which are rewritten through the smokescreen of experience in these books."

"What good is a book if it has no words, or a life not worth living?" I said, looking at my sleeve in horror.

"Now you're getting it, Dan," Hutely muttered while raiding an apple cart on fire.

"Getting what? They must have used Eracermate pens," I said. I couldn't help feeling I was back in history class taking a fill-in-the-blank test. "I got it all right, straight from the animal's snout."

Chang let out a cautious laugh, then said, "At least you wore sleeves. I wasn't so lucky on my last time travel." After her disgusting revelation, Chang retrieved large saddlebags from the smoldering cart. She and I attached the bags to Hutely. They fit Hutely like a glove. Then we placed the books, six in all, in the pouches of the saddlebags.

After Hutely devoured hot apples dripping with pectin, he told us to get on his back. We ducked into a nearby building, entered a hallway, but then climbed a series of stairs to a balcony overlooking the main square. Now that we were safe from Qin soldiers, Hutely explained the details of our mission and the significance of the books.

"You see, Dan, these books represent the five civilizing principles of ancient Chinese thought. These are the Book of Songs, Documents, Changes, Seasonal Annals, and Ceremonial Rituals. They are the essential blueprints for Chinese history and culture. The Qin are looking to rewrite history. Their scribes are busy writing books expounding Legalist ideology. They're promoting Sun Tzu's Art of War and the Seasonal Annals. Being the first dynasty to unify China, they feel they have a decree of heaven or mandate to rule. They obviously don't need people's permission. This will have a ripple effect on history if their literature replaces the original five. In their eyes, the ends justify the means no matter what the cost. People must not lose their precious past. Before the Zhou, the Shang were China's true founding dynasty."

"Okay," I said, trying to make sense of the numbers. "The dragon skin protects the books, but I counted six civilizing books in all. There are three on each side of your saddlebags, Hutely. Weren't there only five that needed saving?" I concluded thoroughly confused.

"The dragons included the Tao Te Ching," Chang said with a hint of elation. "The Seasonal Annals are of keen interest to the Qin, so the dragons spared a copy from the book burning for posterity. The dragons are just being cautious, Dan," Chang answered, leaving Hutely off the yoke.

"We are here at the request of the dragons, Dan," said Hutely, munching an unidentified lying object in a garbled voice. This made Chang laugh.

"Same old Hutely," she said, fist-hoofing him.

"Who are these dragons?" I asked with a real sense of fear as I looked out at the soldiers killing and maiming innocent people. "Where did they come from, and what's our connection to them?" I inquired forcefully, shrugging my shoulders and staring intently at Hutely. But it was Chang who supplied the answers once again. While Hutely kept an eye out on the square below, Chang explained. Kwan Yin and the animals saved all they could and retreated out of sight to fight another day during her explanation.

"All of us Chinese believe we are descended from dragons. Like the Chinese people, they are beloved for their capacity for good. They display a dignity that is admired throughout the prefectures. They are seen as the bringers of joy and miracles," she insisted with a reverent tone.

"Well," I said, pointing to the violence all around us, "we need to witness a miracle about now. That would do us a world of good, don't you think?"

"We have already witnessed miracles, Dan! Don't you think?" she countered.

"Like the ones I see happening outside!"

Along with the book burnings, to quash freedom of thought, Zheng buried 460 scholars alive in the second year of his reign. Mao also targeted scholars during the ill-fated Cultural Revolution and Great Leap Forward.

"Come on, Dan, Kwan Yin and here angels of mercy saved our butts! How about dragon- skinned books that sang to you and Hutely from a fiery inferno. Not to mention the brave tigers who saved the day and might have just saved China's liturgical future!"

Hutely told us to keep it down but asked Chang to continue her lesson on dragons. The noise in the square was deafening and horrifying, but I couldn't imagine our voices being heard by anyone, especially Chang who was rather soft spoken.

"I don't think anyone can hear us, Chang, do you?"

"I can hear you," Hutely snorted sarcastically. I had forgotten that the master mule had super-animal hearing. Chang just smiled and continued her lesson, but not before I took a swipe at Hutely.

"I suppose the saddlebags heard us and are plotting our arrest." Hutely momentarily sniffed at me and swatted me with his tail.

"Oh, they're listening all right," said Chang in a serious tone while putting her hand over my mouth.

"Come now, Chang, I was kidding," I said while gently removing her soft hand from my lips.

"I'm not, the dragons hear us through the books in the saddlebags."

"What, do books have ears?" I asked foolishly.

"Didn't the books sing out a question, 'When love leaves, what takes its place?'" she asked shrugging her shoulders, looking at Hutely.

Hutely hoofed my shoulder and said, "Look closely, Dan. You won't see many men, but there are thousands of miracles scared for their lives in the square. They're dressed in blue, green, and brown coats. They resemble 'Down' coats in your time, Dan. They're also wearing Jin or soft caps. Others have stiff hats that are referred to as Moa. The older folks are in Guan or formal wear. These are loving families that the Qin seek to break up in their anti-aristocratic crusade. The women are Ji and wear their hair long to honor both parents, fathers, and mothers. Their past and future legacies are the miracles we must protect and preserve. We were sent in the name of love to give back what the dragons unselfishly gave up for the Chinese people. Those books are part of the dynastic dragon' s soul.

"Absolutely, Hutely, but how do we do that?" I said, staring at Hutely while Chang gave me a puzzled look.

Hutely and Chang looked at each other and then at me as a light turned on in my worried mind. I finally began to understand the gravity of our situation. In order to save the Millet Ruler, the Duke of Zhou, and Lao Tzu's legacies, the fifth child would encounter helpful people, oracle bones, dragons, gods, and goddesses in certain ancient dynastic periods. Chang (a goddess herself) added that the only way to rewrite the dragon-skinned books is through the God of Five Roads who bridges the gap between the dead and the living. He promotes opportunity and well-being. That was something we really needed given the circumstances.

In an instant, Qin soldiers surrounded the square. In the center of the carnage, there appeared the emperor's entourage. Waves of soldiers cleared the square of bodies, belongings, and humanity. Soldiers erected a makeshift stage in minutes as the emperor, Zheng, took center stage and delivered a justification for the violence. The same violence that was imposed on the same audience he was addressing. He spoke with devilish impunity.

"This is a momentous day for what is to be known as China! I, Zheng who now goes by the name Qin Shi Huang Di, have unified the north, south, east, and west. I am your lord and master! I will soon join Huang Di the Yellow Emperor as one of the immortals. I will drink the 'Elixir of Life'! We both derived order out of chaos. The true Taoist has won, and we have defeated the hereditary lords of Confucian troublemakers. They have made attempts on my life. A foolish warlord sent Jing Ke to stab my heart, but I killed him with my bare hands." At that point, the emperor was shaking. He had a sinister grin on his face as he raised his hands to greet an imaginary figure. Zheng cried out, "Oh brave Qin general, so as your head has rejoined your body, so too has China formed. I can't believe that a foolish blind musician with a lead-filled harp thought he could deny my immortality! Now

I see that Huang Di created orderliness and rose in immortal glory." Zheng, who became known as Qin Shi Huang Di, or first emperor, was feverishly shaking so much, a couple of his courtiers escorted him off.

"This guy is whacked, Hutely," I said, squatting behind Hutely and holding Chang's hand. I then angrily added, "Musicians reflect the mood of the people!"

Chang put her hand over my mouth and whispered, "Keep your voice down and maybe we'll live to hear more dragon-inspired music."

"He can't help himself, Chang," Hutely snorted. "Dan is a musician from turbulent times in his home country's history. In the upcoming twentieth-century United States of America, 1960s musicians like Bob Dylan, Steppenwolf, and the Byrds voiced concerns through music regarding America's empire-building tendencies. American leaders needed to reread their cherished documents for guidance and reaffirm their mandate from heaven."

"Absolutely, Hutely, it's never foolish for people to speak out against a government's oppression and expect them to live up to their moral creed."

"In this case, the oppression warranted the pelting of an official with a lead-filled guitar," said Hutely, gritting, grinding, and gnashing his teeth.

"Absolutely, Hutely. During The Who and Hendrix shows, instruments and the stage usually got the worst of it," I added after removing Chang's fingers from my lips again. "Stop with the grinding, Hutely," I said, shrugging my shoulders to lessen the effect. It was like nails on a chalkboard!

Chang smiled and apologized for muzzling me. She then said, "I am a Taoist. Zheng pretends the way of the Tao, but he thinks of his own legacy. Heeding the bird's call or the wolf's howl sounds like a clever idea to me, but he has no justification for his actions and especially for the killing of his people."

Qin soldiers reestablished order after clearing out hecklers from the crowd. After the emperor was in his royal chariot, a second speaker took the stage. He, like Zheng, wore flowing robes filled with borders and round designs that resembled gardens and nature scenes. He was Li Si, the Grand Councilor of Qin, senior advisor to Shi Huang Di, who, according to Hutely, was responsible for many of the sweeping changes the first Chinese empire introduced. He walked on the stage carrying a ceremonial sleeve in his right hand and a seal of the state in his left hand. Li Si walked up to a newly placed table and put the sleeve on it. Courtiers brought an ink box to the table. Li Si dipped the seal in the ink and stamped the sleeve. Li Si addressed the crowd.

"We united a divided land full of feudal lords who confused the people with the necessity of antiquity. They remain silent at court but stir rebellion in the streets against the emperor. These depressing descendants of nobility whose mothers corrupted courts will be silenced. The great Legalist Shang Yang from Wei came to Qin and showed Duke Xiao the true way. His clear, strict rules reformed the fractured warring states and created our great Qin Empire! From now on, we are a Meritocracy! Incompetent relatives will no longer be allowed to corrupt the system under the Qin. The Zhou's lands lost the Mandate of Heaven to the mighty Qin!"

"Why don't you sneeze on that sleeve, Hutely," I said half joking. Chang looked ready to muzzle me again, so I quickly kept my tongue and remained silent.

A great commotion was heard from outside the square, which gave Li Si pause. He signaled to his generals to proceed while a broad smile animated his stern face. "Lead the invited yet so-called aristocratic scholars in," he told a ranking Qin soldier. Scholars from all over the countryside were marched in front of the emperor's temporary viewing stand. They were made up of fathers and sons, cousins, and aristocratic family members. They were versed in the Confucian Classics and believed they walked with their worshiped ancestors in all they did. All the while, previously slain city scholars were removed and done away with. Only women, girls, and able-bodied young men were left to witness the next grizzly act of family fragmentation imposed by the Qin administration.

Chapter 3

· · · · · · · · · · · ·

The Magic Ferry

Old and middle-aged male scholars were told to step forward away from distraught family members. Shocked women and children were herded with previous survivors while the scholars were once again executed and carted off. "Taoists aren't like this," Chang said with tears in her eyes.

"But Legalists are. They hide behind the veil of civilized Confucianism and Taoism. A deception that hopefully won't last long," Fu Su said, appearing from behind a curtain and peeling off a green-hooded cloak, which he placed on Hutely's back. Chang ran to him, and they embraced passionately.

Fu Su was an impressive man. He had long black hair that was tied back in a ponytail which reached his waist. His handsome face and hazel eyes were complemented by a slight mustache that brought out his light golden, yellowish complexion. He wore royal robes under his peasant disguise. His broad shoulders were covered by a long maroon coat that extended inches past his knees. His lapel had a wide gray border that looked like connected labyrinths that turned into lotus flowers around his collar. Underneath was an off-white gauze toga that covered yellow trousers which fell over silk sandals. Yellow was reserved for the royal family.

Fu Su was indeed royalty and Zheng's oldest son. He was the rightful heir to the Qin throne. His mother, who was from the state of Zheng, used to sing a local ballad in praise of her son when he was just a boy: "On the Mountains Are Good Trees." Fu Su became synonymous with "Good Tree." So much so, people looked up to him. He was a great warrior but was also merciful, honest, and just. The people loved him even as he won crucial victories for the Qin. Despite his instrumental role in the Qin's rise to power, his father grew tired of his sympathetic and empathetic flaws and attributed his benevolence to weakness. Besides, he was openly opposing Zheng's murderous plans. He was a benevolent Confucianist pitted against his father's malevolent Legalism under the guise of Taoism.

Having had quite enough from his eldest, Zheng sent Fu Su to the harsh northern frontier to supervise General Meng Tian's army in Shangjun. Hu Hai, Zheng's second oldest, and Li Si changed the emperor's will and cut Fu Su out. They sent word to General Ming Tian that he was a failure and needed to commit suicide. A second letter, written by Li Si, instructed Fu Su to poison himself to avoid shaming the emperor. After a short appeal process that failed, Meng fell on his sword, but Fu Su fled to meet up with Master Hutely.

Fu Su and Chang's embrace seemed to last forever. Hutely must have seen me staring. "Fu Su and Chang are a couple, Dan," Hutely seemed to snicker, showing me a full rack of teeth.

"Oh... yeah, I know that," I said in an awkward defensive tone. He's a prince, I thought to myself, feeling a bit common.

"Well, Danny boy, he is a prince, and she is a goddess," Hutely quietly remarked as if reading my mind again.

"Absolutely, Hutely, and I'm a lowly peasant and you're a wandering ass with tenure," I answered back for spite.

"Now that's the spirit... what?" Hutely sputtered as his congenial disposition went south. He would have opened a can of hoof-ass on me if we weren't in so much danger. Fu Su let out a slight laugh as Chang, drying her eyes, managed a labored smile. I on the other hand thought it was very funny. I admire Hutely, but sometimes heehaw needs hindsight.

Hutely wasn't one to hold grudges, and Fu Su suggested that we leave and move to safer ground. Chang and I jumped on Hutely's back as Fu Su sprinted ahead, down the stairs and into a back alley. Lining the alley was a lengthy line of oxcarts attended by Qin transport guards. They recognized Fu Su and bowed in his presence. Hutely kept a safe distance, but he could hear every word they said. "The carts are ready for transport, my lord," the head guard said with a befuddled look on his face.

"We didn't know you were here," added another guard.

"The emperor is sick, and feeble, and needs my help. You mustn't tell anyone you saw me. Not even Master Li Si or my brother is to know. Quickly now, take the chidao to Hao and then Feng. Drop off a cart's worth of clothes and supplies at each post along the way. Then take the remaining twelve carts down the tributary on junks south to the Chang Jang and await your orders," Fu Su quietly commanded.

Without detection, we watched the carts leave over the horizon heading southwest. Fu Su then commandeered the last cart in the caravan. He instructed Chang and I to put on the peasant clothes and stay hidden in the cart. Hutely pulled us out of sight at an alarming rate of speed while Fu Su held the reins.

During their recent romantic reunion, Fu Su told Chang what the plan was, so she shared it with me as we hung on for dear life. Our oxcart sure could have used some shocks as we rambled over rough ground parallel to the Wei He River, going west. Chang told me of a magic ferry up ahead that would take us where we needed to go. Of course, Hutely knew what lay ahead.

In a brief time, we arrived at the magic ferry. It was unlike any ferry I'd ever seen. It was seriously red with a pentagon shape that was surrounded by a golden pulsating electric cage fence and roof. The water underneath it was black, rippling and bubbling up at the surface. Swimming in the black water was a huge jade-colored snake. The last thing I wanted to do was get on that ferry and Hutely knew it. "Okay, Danny boy, hop on my back and we'll board the ferry together."

"Shouldn't someone stay with the oxcart?" I said, staring in disbelief at the jade snake. Hutely saw that I was fixated on the reptile that could easily take me for a delicious snack.

"Don't be afraid, Dan, we are among friends."

"I've never considered snakes my friends, especially ones that make an anaconda look like just another worm." The master mule couldn't help but let out a crazy laugh that sounded like a heehaw on steroids. With Hutely's laughing-choppers on full display, Chang and Fu Su let out a couples' chuckle while hiding their faces. Being the only sane one who wasn't cracking up, I noticed the ferry's electric facade was growing dimmer, revealing the opulent operator.

The operator was dressed in royalty attire with a light green robe and a yellow-striped border lapel that formed a V shape around his long black beard. It continued after a brief interruption by his red belt. The lapel extended, eventually hugging his feet. His loose, cavernous sleeves had the same yellow border as his lapel. Within the yellow borders were red interconnecting squares. With one hand on a golden rudder and the other on a gleaming golden sword, he motioned us to wait before we came aboard. That was fine by me!

With a nod from Hutely, after he stopped heehawing, Fu Su explained the soon-to-be over "Warring States Period" while we waited.

"There were many casualties of the Warring States Period from 475 to 221 BCE, Dan. Royalty and peasants alike were brutalized as states fought for control. During the longest dynasty in Chinese history that was controlled by Zhou leaders, Knights made a remarkable transformation. Once at the bottom of the social order, knights began to slowly take on a greater leadership role."

"Didn't the Zhou have the 'Mandate of Heaven'?" I asked, full knowing that Confucius and Lao Tsu lived earlier in the Zhou's reign.

"That's right, Danny boy," Hutely weighed in. "However, there were independent states that made up the Zhou Dynasty. They included the states of Yan, Chu, Han, and Wei. After the relatively peaceful Spring and Autumn period, nobles in these states stopped supporting the Zhou. Some say that the Zhou needed to exert more control instead of letting the states fend for themselves. More powerful states dominated others until the Qin finally won out overall."

"Knights filled the positions left by ousted family-related nobles of the aristocracy. They gained the necessary administrative experience to oversee state activities in the area of road building, agriculture—you need food to feed an army—and finally, state expansion at the expense of their neighbors," Fu Su added as we turned our attention to the impressive ferry operator.

"So you see, Dan, we are here also to preserve the Spring and Autumn period for posterity so they may know peace instead of just Legalism tyranny," Chang concluded as the ferry operator was now fully visible and began telling his story.

"My name is Chu Yuan. I was once a powerful and highly respected diplomat to King Huai of Chu. I set up strategic alliances between my warring neighbors, and I tried to promote peace by exposing rampant corruption in the various state courts. The corrupted and powerful King Hui of Qin persuaded King Huai to demote me and break up my bridge-building alliances. After my banishment, I authored poems that expanded verses in the pursuit of good governance along with other justifiable prose. Now my nine poems are in danger of being lost forever at the hands of my nemesis, the Qin. The Jade Emperor has called on me to be your conductor through time and the underworld."

"Greetings, Chu Yuan," Hutely whinnied, motioning all of us to bow. After the greeting ceremony, we were invited on board. Chu Yuan lowered a plank for us to walk across. The magic ferry floor was white and gleamed in the sun.

"Wipe your feet, Dan," Hutely commanded in a jovial voice.

"Very funny. I'm on your back, remember. Wipe your hooves, wise ass," I said, which elicited a stern look from Chu Yuan. After I covered my mouth, Chu Yuan gestured that I dismount before entering. Chang, Fu Su, and Hutely entered and walked onto the starchy-looking floor of the ferry. It looked like it was covered in rice paper. After taking a deep breath, I took one step and then another. It was like the floor wasn't there. I suddenly felt light as a feather. "Why do I feel like I'm on the moon, Hutely?"

"Only those with good intentions feel like they're devoid of gravity, Dan. If you would have left footsteps, well, you didn't, and we'll leave it at that."

"Absolutely, Hutely! But why rice?"

"I'll tell you why, Dan," Chu Yuan said in a sad tone. "I was so distraught that my beloved state of Chu had been taken over by the Qin, I tied myself to a rock and jumped into the Milou River. Grieving villagers sailed their boats and tried to search for my body. They beat drums and smacked the current with their oars to scare off hungry fish. Finally, they threw rice as a sacrifice to my spirit. The very same rice that now covers the ferry floor."

There were bright yellow benches that lined the sides of the ferry. Fu Su, Chang, and I sat down and tried to relax. But we all felt an anxious anticipation over where it would dock next. Fu Su felt a kindred spirit with Chu Juan and explained that he too tried to head off the tide of corruption and intolerance his deranged father was currently causing. Furthermore, that he was ordered by his father to drink poison and commit suicide. "Luckily, Hutely appeared to me in a dream and asked me to travel time with him," said Fu Su with a bowing gesture.

"Thank you for coming here, Prince," Hutely said, bowing his head. Meanwhile, I felt sorry for Chu Yuan, and somehow his story was familiar to me.

"Gee, Chu Yuan's story rings a bell somehow," I said in a faint voice.

"I'm not surprised, Dan," said Hutely while backing up and sitting half his carcass on a bench. "You see, Dan, on the fifth day of the fifth month of every year in China, they pay homage to Chu Yuan by celebrating the Dragon Boat Festival. In your time, Danny boy, the Communist Party considers Chu Yuan a hero-patriot and the 'people's poet' for his anti-corruption work and ultimate sacrifice for the state he loved."

"Absolutely, Hutely! His sacrifice reminds me of Socrates' refusal to flee after he was convicted of corrupting the youth of Athens. He could have skipped town, but his followers were ready to help him!"

"If I remember correctly," Hutely said, pointing the hoof at me, "you wanted to help him do just that, Danny boy. Didn't you?"

"Don't remind me," I said, feeling a little guilty.

With that said, Chu Yuan put his hand on my shoulder and said, "I took my life as a matter of principle. I couldn't live while the Qin reign of terror lit my ideals and life's work up in flames. Thankfully, because of all your efforts"—Chu Yuan bowed to each of us while a tear rolled down his cheek—"Jia Yi from Luoyang will write a poem and resurrect my Lament and Chinese patriotism through the centuries." He especially thanked Hutely with a pet of his mane and a couple of rice bowls which Hutely hoovered up in a hurry. Unbeknownst to us, a huge Jade Dragon had replaced the considerably smaller snake. It appeared suddenly and started our descent down to the God of Five Roads or Wu Toa.

The Jade Dragon wrapped around the ferry with its giant magnificent face looking at us while its tail swung around as we plunged downward. Its body glowed green and its face resembled a cross between a wicked elk, alligator, and a revered dinosaur. Rectangular chunks of its tail's skin were missing. Electric, pulsating grid-graphs filled the spaces of displaced skin. Hutely's saddlebags began vibrating wildly as the dragon book covers longed to rejoin their mother's tail. The benevolent dragon spoke to the written glory of the dragon's utility and longevity through the ages.

"The dragon dances in spring festivals while originating rains saturate regions. Suppress the rebellious insect carnivals who incite the ever-present diseases. Han unrestrained and magnificent. Tang, gentle, graceful, and tamed. Song, delicate with flowers they became. Protruding foreheads signify wisdom and longevity antlers evolve such kingdoms. Ox's ear successful examination couple with tiger-eyed power and rising sun. Eagle claws its bravery soaring, fish-tail flexibility splashing. Horse's teeth reveal diligence passing. The dragon dances in a new morning."

We splashed down on an underground river that was surrounded by a green glowing well. Chu Yuan boarded the Jade Dragon and flew up through the misty air and disappeared.

"Where do they think they're going?" I yelled, which echoed green light as I spoke.

"They're going back up to meet us," Hutely whinnied, full knowing that I would feel abandoned and slightly confused. "We have forty-nine days to complete the books and rejoin the dragon skin with its mother, Danny boy."

"What if it takes fifty days or maybe just a couple of days?" I added hoping for an easy explanation. Fu Su and Chang just smiled as they both jumped from the ferry and onto the misty shore. Hutely walked off and started munching on a patch of green glowing, globular, and gooey vegetation. "Hutely, your belly is glowing green!"

"Relax, Dan, it helps with digestion, and it makes me..."

"Absolutely, Hutely! You got that right," I gasped while vacating the immediate area. After that dreadful poop sighting and smell, I got my answer.

Chapter 4

. . . .

Ancient Chinese Evolution Theater

"That depends on how well you are received by the ancestor souls of the underworld, Dan," a softly spoken, lone voice cried out through the mist. It was Tu Ti the God of the Earth and spokesperson for the God of Five Roads. He was small in stature and his jade robe glowed earth tones as he spoke. Tu Ti looked a little gaunt, and he was slightly hunched over with long slicked-back white hair accompanied by a sparse pointed beard. His deep-set eyes bulged a little with each change of his facial expression.

"How did you know my name?" I asked cautiously.

"Hutely said you were coming," Tu Ti explained while petting Hutely's mane, not seeming to care what lay a few feet away. "Thank you for your fertile gift, my friend," he said, smiling at Hutely. He then started explaining how he knew I was coming. "You are the fifth child and are descended from brave warriors. Your father's Lunar Module work for *Apollo* propelled people through space. This inspired time travel. You were born in the year of the rat, meaning you know how to survive," he concluded, motioning me to exit the magic ferry.

"Another gift awaits you when he sneezes; but make sure your sleeve is all the way down," I said earnestly, which drew a sneer and a hoof stomp from Hutely.

"Ha... ha... and he even has an American sense of humor to boot!"

"So you know about Americans?" I asked with a smile.

"Compared to China, America, or better yet the USA, was not that old when you were born, Dan. The Chinese and Americans often

23

have found common ground through negotiation, trade, and mutual understanding," Tu Ti said to a lighted blue-green accompaniment.

"I see some similarities between America and China," I added enthusiastically. Tu Ti and Hutely exchanged glances as if to say later, or earlier in time for that matter. "Now... now.... hear me out!" I started to sound like Hutely. He was starting to rub off on me, which was better than him rubbing up against me. "America's two major political parties resemble two prominent Chinese schools of thought," I said. By this time Chang and Fu Su had joined the conversation and were looking at me with skeptical anticipation.

"Well," Hutely said with a devilish puzzle to his muzzle. Tu Ti glowed his approval for my acquiescent proposition.

"In my time, Republicans, like Taoists here, feel less government is better. They even think that government may be the root of societal problems in general. Republicans believe the hidden hand of the deity will justifiably intervene, while Taoists believe nature-based solutions are better than Confucian rigidity." Everyone seemed to give me a tired look as Hutely let out a mighty yawn.

"An American sense of humor also has a valid point," said Tu Ti with an impressive light show. "Please continue, Dan," said Tu Ti.

"Okay," I said, feeling validated. "Democrats, like practitioners of Confucianism, feel government and public officials have an obligation to improve the lot of others in society. They feel a noble calling to initiate a man-made solution for issues of poverty, hunger, and human despair. Like young Confucian illegitimate sons of courtly concubines who went out in harm's way to help others, Democrats too had people who risked everything to make society a better place." I was giving the brightest seventies disco ball a run for its money at this point. "Why, Martin Luther King, Cesar Chavez, Delores Huerta, and Robert F. Kennedy tried to solve societal ills. All faced jail time while two were even assassinated." A reverent hum was suddenly heard throughout the well.

"The earthly souls of the five roads bless the mission you must take with Hutely, Fu Su, and Chang," said a bowing Tu Ti who now resembled a Lava lamp with appendages.

"Now, both schools of thought face Legalist aggression," Fu Su added, squeezing Chang's hand firmly.

"All of us and the books are heading for a lesson that starts from the beginning and will include a fourth school of thought," Hutely said while shooing us back on the magic ferry.

"What? We just got off, Hutely," I yelled, acting like a child. Chang and Fu Su each grabbed an arm and lifted me back on the ferry.

"They had to make sure you weren't a barbarian, Dan," Chang said, smiling and squeezing my hand.

"It's really a compliment," Fu Su added, reclaiming Chang's hand.

"Consider your passport stamped, Danny boy. Now just watch, listen, and learn," Hutely instructed with a sense of urgency. "We need to sit on the benches and hold on." If you haven't seen a donkey sitting on a bench and holding on with its hooves, you haven't lived!

"You must now ride the ancient whirlwind of Chinese evolution," Tu Ti exclaimed as he rose up through the well, causing it to spin. We rose as if we were in the eye of a storm. Images started appearing all around us as if in a 360-degree cylinder theater.

"What, no popcorn or Milk Duds?"

"Quiet, Dan!" Hutely whinnied wildly as our world changed drastically. Tu Ti started narrating what we were seeing, or lack thereof.

"Within the empty primordial chaos, an egg was hatched. Earth and Pangu existed in a state of unity within this black age." Well, you guessed it. It was hard to see. I did see Hutely who looked freaked out. Could it be that the master mule is afraid of the dark? Go figure. Fu Su and Chang held each other tight, but looking all around as if waiting for something scary to happen. It all made me hungry and an unlikely role reversal for Hutely and I. Go figure, again. He must have had an upset stomach from the squishy green thing he ate. Anyway, Tu Ti continued his narration.

"Pangu broke the egg creating heaven and earth. He separated the Yin from the Yang with an ax blow. Yin, the heavier, sank and became earth, while Yang, the lighter, rose to form the sky. Pangu held them together for eighteen hundred years and while resting afterward:

His breath blew wind with a thundering voice.

His eyes beheld the Sun and Moon.

His body became mountains and his blood, rivers.

His skin formed ground, bones, and minerals.

His marrow created sacred stones and his sweat fell as rain.

After Pangu rested, the goddess Nuwa formed humans out of yellow clay.

Individually crafting smart humans, but then grew tired, dripping mud from a rope instead; thus, forming lesser humans."

As I looked at the others, they were all staring at me. "What's up, Hutely, Fu Su, Chang, is something wrong?"

"Oh no, we're good," they said, assuring each other. This could have something to do with my attitude before the lights went out. But now the lights were on, and I could see the saddlebags vibrating. Our surroundings of glorious earth and sky quickly advanced through neolithic times when farming became prevalent, and people settled down with domesticated animals. The Millet Ruler rose from ruts in the soil to feed the people.

"Now... that's what I'm talking about!" I yelled as if at a drive-in movie. Tu Ti laughed but continued his narration.

"Xia Dynasty starts divination by fire through three sovereigns and five emperors. Oracle bone scripts on animal bones and tortoise shells answer questions of dynastic change. The god Shang-ti grants us a glimpse into the ancient Shang world." A chorus of musical imagery suddenly filled our circular, ancient Chinese theater.

> *Cities of the Shang, cities of the Shang.*
> *Inscriptions in bone, inscriptions in bone and stone.*
> *Defeated by the Zhou, in a feudal somehow.*
> *A family of kings pulling the strings.*
> *Descended from the Millet Ruler.*
> *Cities of the Shang, elephants in war.*
> *Silkworms spinning thread, weaving silk cloth.*
> *Kaolin clay, bronze displays.*
> *A family of kings, merrily sings.*
> *Metal in the decree of heaven.*
> *Movements of the moon, ten-day cycles in tune.*
> *Priests added days, the king's harvest praised.*
> *Characters in thirds, pull-iron-stone magnets.*
> *Gives meaning to all, in the decree of heaven.*

Cities of the Shang, elephants in war.
Silkworms spinning thread, weaving silk cloth.
Kaolin clay, bronze displays.
A family of kings merrily sings.
Metal in the decree of heaven.

We were all captivated by the images spinning around us described in the song. Hutely's saddlebags danced to the music, and they would have made John Travolta jealous. Like the Dave Clark Five sang, everyone else seemed "glad all over." Chang and Fu Su chose to slow-dance while Hutely did a four-legged waltz. Being not much of a dancer, I focused on the lyrics. "Why such a confused look, Dan?" Hutely whinnied while waltzing wonderfully.

"Well," I said, "I get the song like adding days to the calendar. The king's harvest praised of course leads to affirming the decree of heaven. Having elephants in war didn't hurt their territorial aspirations, which always leads to artistic, cultural exchange. But what does 'Pull-iron-stone magnets' mean? I've heard of pull chicken, or 'you're pulling my leg,' but what the cluck?" Hutely's chainsaw laugh echoed through and bounced around the theater.

"You see, Dan," Hutely said, halting his high-powered heehaw, "the ancient Chinese were one of the few peoples who developed a unique written language. First off, Chinese words were just one syllable. To express more complicated meanings, they combined characters, words, or syllables together."

"Absolutely, Hutely. They used pictures of characters that made it easier for their neighbors to understand and learn Chinese, right? I mean, they could understand the pictures," I said, clarifying my meaning.

"That's correct, Dan, but let's concentrate on your question to better understand the development of Chinese writing and language. They developed in essence compound words like characters in thirds or pull-iron-stone to mean magnet.

"Oh, right... but I don't understand how the written characters relate to spoken Chinese," I said out loud, "especially since the Historical Guide Academy made it so I could understand Chinese speakers and they could understand me."

"Well, Danny boy, maybe this will help," Hutely said. "Through many years of development, ideograms and phonograms replaced pictographs."

"Absolutely, Hutely. Wow! I thought video and phonographs were originally developed in Menlo Park, New Jersey, by Thomas Edison; instead, they were Chinese innovations? Unbelievable, aye, Hutely?"

"Yes, Dan. What you thought is unbelievable!" Hutely whinnied angrily. "What I meant was that Chinese characters have two parts. One is the idea sign, or clue to the meaning of the character. In other words, like I said before, the ideogram." Another hard to believe fact was the all-knowing ass was still doing the four-legged waltz as he continued the lesson. "The other was the phonetic or sound sign to help pronounce the character." Hutely then told me that a man named Cangjie invented Chinese writing. It gave him immense pleasure noting that Cangjie observed animals (of course) and specifically the footprints of birds and their claw marks. Well, my response, foolishly, was that it was hard to verify.

"Didn't he also observe natural phenomena?"

"Yes, he did, Danny boy, but a closer look at his calligraphy reveals strong animal input."

"Absolutely, Hutely!"

Hutely and I were so lost in our conversation about language, we didn't notice our theater was now just an everyday run-of-the-mill water well. Our ferry was like an earthen ship floating at the bottom. Gone were the benches, but a tree sprouted up through the middle. Its horizontal branches grew and led the way through the mist. Fu Su had us grab hold of the tree limbs, which guided us in the right direction. Two good trees had made an amazing natural connection.

Once off the ferry, the mist cleared, giving us a better view of our surroundings. Hutely told us we had just passed through the first road which ran through the well and into the underworld. We had four more to travel and pass through to successfully fulfill our mission the H. G. Academy sent us on.

"Hey, speaking of the well, and the tree, where did they go? Tu Ti... Tu Ti," I called out again, but he was gone too.

"Don't worry, Danny boy, we'll see the Jade Dragon, Chu Yuan, and Tu Ti again. The souls of the earth of the Chinese 'Way' have given us the green light to the next road," Hutely assured me while flipping me onto his back with his snout. Fu Su was giving Chang a piggyback ride as we made our way down a dirt road out of the mist and into sunlight. It appeared to me that Chang liked being serenaded to by Fu Su who was humming a tune.

"Stop staring, Dan," Hutely whispered as if not to disturb the happy couple's bliss.

"Oh, sorry, Hutely," I said longingly as Hutely swung his tail across my shoulder.

"Don't worry, Dan. Someday soon you'll find your own ship of love and sail off with that special someone."

"Guess so," I said softly, but soon I began to wonder why the Shang's mandate of heaven ended.

"It's a shame the Shang showed what a dynasty should do and then not so much," Hutely sighed.

"Okay, Hutely, what's that supposed to mean?" I asked confusedly.

"You see, Dan, a new dynasty will emerge in the State of Lu, and we are tasked to document the happenings there so it won't be lost to history. The Sage of Lu, commonly known as the Duke of Zhou, will face the challenges of a fractured family and an emerging dynasty in peril."

"Absolutely, Hutely, and they would be the Zhou Dynasty who produced much of what we're trying to save, right? He also inspired Confucius if I'm not mistaken." Without answering me, Hutely asked me to scratch the top of his massive right leg. I held my breath, then we traveled on.

Chapter 5

. . . .

Muscle-Power Technology

The first people we encountered were farmers working in their fields. There were oxcarts with iron plows tilling the land which would bring in a harvest of mostly barley, millet, and wheat. The Chinese New Year was in the rear-view mirror and spring had sprung. There was a wide canal that ran north which stemmed from a huge reservoir created by a dike near the Huang He River.

Our time travel had sent us back eight hundred years to the early Zhou Dynasty near the Louyang plain due west at Fenghao around 1100 BCE. It was fairly close to where I had met up with Hutely during the future Qin Dynasty around 210 BCE. We were in the fabled state of Lu, and challenges lay ahead.

In the Yellow River region with flooding and loess brown silt build up, the flooding was both a blessing and a curse. The loess soil would build up, thus, damming rivers, which made future floods unpredictably dangerous and life threatening. Such occurrences brought farmers, villages, and royalty together. An ever-increasing population led to the accentuation of a communal muscle-power technology out of necessity.

Fu Su and Chang knew two of the farmers in charge of irrigation. Many of their fields were carved into hillsides and needed water pumped up to different levels.

"What the heck is that, Hutely?" I asked with fascination and wonder.

"It's a chain pump called a 'Dragon Backbone,' Dan. It's a wooden frame that extends down to a water source, it is a form of treadle pump. The ancient Persians and Minoans also used these pumps."

"I don't remember seeing one," I said, trying to remember Greek farming techniques.

"Yeah... you tend to miss things, but let's move on," Hutely said with a slight heehaw. "Do you see those pedals on the lower part of the upper frame turning that long horizontal shaft, Dan?"

"Absolutely, Hutely. It's like they're riding a bike and pulling those buckets of water uphill. You know, that looks like fun, Hutely!"

"Fun?" Hutely retorted, but then added, "I've been strapped to mechanical wheels usually reserved for oxen. It's crazy work even for a donkey with strong legs like mine." Hutely went on to explain that muscle-power technology has served China well over the centuries and is still in use today. Handheld plows and oxen are used in rice production because of hilly, terraced slopes that modern machinery can't reach. Furthermore, rice is sown by hand and covered in ashes. A transplant team collects rice seedlings into bundles of straw and fertilizer. He went on to say that the Shang imported rice from the south that had a wet climate as opposed to the north's dry weather.

"Do you think they'd let me try, Hutely?"

"Come over here, Dan," Fu Su and Chang said in unison. One of the peddlers got off the treadle pump and motioned for me to get on. I did without hesitation and began peddling. I should have noticed how incredibly fit the peddlers were before climbing aboard.

"Now try to keep up, friend. We need to tread water up to this field," Shi said as he peddled faster and faster. "Teng is the fastest peddler in the kingdom. He'll be sad if we fall behind, and so will I."

"What's the rush, Shi?" I asked, panting, and finding it hard to keep up.

"Well, Dan. It is Dan, right?" Shi asked with a smirk while extending his hand and giving me a high-five.

"Yes, it is," I said, wondering if the high-five started in ancient China.

"Our village has people who depend on us farmers to till, plant, water, and harvest the millet, barley, and wheat so they won't starve and go hungry. If we don't succeed, they might starve to death. There are stiff penalties that could be inflicted on us if that happens."

"Oh... what penalties?"

"It has been said that a farmer, years ago, and his family oversaw irrigating lower fields. His son accidentally flooded them out and ruined the harvest. Many starved and died for lack of food."

"What happened to the son, Shi?"

"The whole family was shamed, executed, and dismembered. Their extremities were hung in the town square for all to see." My eyes widened, and any feeling of hunger disappeared.

"Isn't that kind of harsh?" I replied, feeling my arms and legs cramping. Shi nodded and stopped pedaling as Teng climbed up the dragon's backbone and relieved me. We hadn't moved much water up hill. I was very happy to get off, but I didn't want anyone to think I was wimping out. "Back so soon, Teng?" I said, gesturing that I could continue.

"Yes, Dan," he said with a smile, gripping the overhead beam. "I was only taking five. Thanks for pedaling! We wouldn't want the new dynasty's regent, Dan, to have any more problems to deal with."

"Well," I said, totally misreading the meaning of Teng's comment, "you know... all in a day's work, guys," I added humbly. Shi and Teng looked at each other and let out rapturous laughs while pedaling at warp speed. I must have looked like a stick figure making my way back toward Hutely who was shaking his head and chewing his cud. "Don't say it! I know how pathetic that was. I should have taken your advice, Hutely."

"They admired your enthusiasm and willingness to dive in feet first without hesitation, Dan. You displayed a classic American spirit that is refreshing. No matter what the odds against you, you give it all you got. That includes your regent duties too." With that said, Fu Su and Chang burst out laughing, trying desperately to hold back the tears.

"What's so funny?" I said, cracking a confused smile. What no one would tell me is that the new regent of the Zhou Dynasty was also named Dan. He became known as the Duke of Zhou.

"I'll explain later, Dan, all in good time," Hutely hooted, but desperately trying hard to keep his chainsaw in check while giving the tearful duo a weird look. I didn't mind all the jocularity, especially after witnessing Legalist aggression by the Qin. After a round of bathroom stops and a quick grazing session, Hutely once again pulled us along in the mule cart toward Fenghao. I started noticing all the muscle power modes of mobility that were coming and going all around us.

"Hey, would you look at all those crazy contraptions cruising to and from the next town, Hutely," I said, still wondering what was so funny. "That looks like a whole family jammed into a sort of wheelbarrow and being pushed by poor laborers. They must be a royal family, aye, Hutely."

"Very good, Danny boy, you are correct. Wheelbarrows served as the upper class's family car. They are more efficient than western wheelbarrows with the wheels balanced over each side of the axle. As you can see, the family is pushed easily by servants.

"Wow, there's another, and another. Look! Coming towards us are three with sails riding the wind!" Chang and Fu Su smiled and acknowledged our increasing traffic.

"Look at that line of Palanquins, Dan," Chang said, turning my head in their direction. "The royals use them to and from the burial grounds. Ancestor worship was strong through the early dynasties."

"Penguins? Where? They must be imported from Antarctica!" Upon hearing my latest misunderstanding, Hutely reared up and brought our mule cart to an abrupt stop.

"Palanquin, Dan! They are also known as Sedan Chairs," said Hutely, shaking his mane.

"Absolutely, Hutely, but those servants must get tired of supporting those poles. But you must admit, those are stylish boxes the royals travel in. They remind me of the one in ancient Egypt that Queen Nefretiri rode in, aye, Hutely?"

"Yes, Dan," Hutely whinnied irritably, tightening the cart and mule attachments that loosened during his quick stop. "Muscle power was prominent in the ancient world and especially in China, Dan," he said, lightening up a bit. "The Jinrikisha was replaced by the Pedicab with the invention of ball bearings and used well into the twentieth century on Chinese roads. Like the treadle pump, it required human effort for pedaling. High-speed rail and electricity will lessen the need for muscle-power technology," Hutely concluded, but not wanting to see too far into my future.

"What are penguins, Dan?" Chang inquired jovially, putting her hand over Fu Su's mouth.

"Well," I said looking at Fu Su, shaking my head in sympathy and solidarity, "they're cute little aquatic animals that mate for life and look like they're wearing tuxedos, or better yet, royal outfits." Overhearing us, Hutely let out a large grunt.

"If we pass through Antarctica, do point them out, Dan," Chang added after initiating a slap fight with her royal bow.

"Looks like they have giant moles here, Hutely," I said. If there are huge dragons, then it stands to reason the moles might be big as well. Made good sense to me.

"Absolutely not, Danny boy. Those are burial sites like Chang mentioned," Hutely reinformed me while swatting flies with his tail but missing them and striking me.

"Hutely! Stop with the tail, already."

"Keep the flies away and I'll stop."

"Dan, catch," Chang said as she threw me an accordion fan. While performing my fly-swatting duty, I realized just how vast the burial sites were. I had no way of knowing just how much they would come into play while on our mission. Hutely went on to explain that former kings had their entourages buried with them. Generations of royalty really filled up the place. The town's burial ground was like a huge rectangle that surrounded the outskirts of the city. It held both Shang and newly buried Zhou royalty.

Chapter 6

· · · · · · · · · · · · ·

Song the Young King

"Hey, Hutely, is this guy... Dan, as important as I think he is?" I asked, knowing he was.

"The Duke of Zhou's legacy will be in these saddlebags, my boy," Hutely answered, obviously in the mood for a long biographical tirade. "We'll meet him and maybe the young king when we enter the royal courtyard," Hutely said while looking for a place to graze. His stomach once again took precedent over historical analysis. Not finding a good spot nearby, we high-tailed it and ox-carted past the inner boundary of the burial sites through the city's outer walls. Then we passed through a shiny bronze gate that resembled a tangle of tree branches that led into a residential area.

As Hutely hung his head and ate scraps that fell off carts coming in from the farms, Fu- Su, Chang, and I walked around the peasant streets just outside an industrial area. The residential dwellings were anything but palatial. They had pounded earth foundations that supported rectangular, square, and oval timber frames. The walls were mud-packed around rough stones that when dried could withstand harsh weather. They had thatched roofs composed of straw and reed bundles supported by wooden poles.

Each dwelling faced south with an inner courtyard. According to Hutely, even though these dwellings are small, their courtyards serve the same ceremonial functions as the regent's royal abode. Similar ceremonies are performed from the lowest peasant to the highest royal in their courtyards, thus, giving the citizens a feeling of normalcy, continuity, and inner peace. Keeping the peace is important around here. Hutely also said this was a good example of homogeneity, or where everyone has a similar ethnicity and knows what everybody else is doing.

As Fu Su and Chang helped a couple of elderly ladies hang laundry, Hutely finished his morning meal and shared it with me.

"You see, Dan," said Hutely, talking with his mouth full and dripping remnants of his snack on my sandals.

"Absolutely, Hutely, I see that the academy failed in teaching you table manners and proper hygiene." While I was speaking to Hutely, one of the elderly ladies snatched my sandals from underneath me and replaced them with another pair in one fell swoop. She washed my soiled sandals, and Fu Su hung them on the line. Two elderly couples who were sweeping their courtyards rushed over, led Hutely to a horse trough, and scrubbed his hideous hide. Chang shielded his eyes from the soap while Hutely heehawed his disapproval. He was so full of soap he resembled a yeti in deep snow. Everyone was laughing with big smiles except Hutely who looked like he didn't get the joke. For the first time in our travels, I felt sorry for the embarrassed equine. Five seniors ran over with water vessels and gave Hutely a thorough rinsing.

Just when I thought things couldn't get any more bizarre, around twenty screaming toddlers and several moms, donning towels, descended on Hutely. He looked like a papier-mâché monster with moving parts. They dried him off quickly and left screaming away with their moms back to whence they came.

"What was that all about?" I asked. "These people must have an impeccable sense of smell. I can understand Hutely's wetting, but my sandals?"

"Look at your new sandals, Dan," Fu Su directed while embracing Chang.

"They're yellowish gold," I said, liking the look of them.

"They're also the color of royalty, Dan," said Chang while pointing to Fu Su's royal undergarments. Fu Su was quick to close his peasant coat to avoid detection. "We're on our way to the royal court and we must be dressed appropriately and smell good," she chuckled, causing Hutely to let out a loud groan. "After all, we're not barbarians," she said, still chuckling.

"You mean all these peasants and children knew we had a date with the emperor?" I said, scratching my head.

After gaining a bit of his composure back, Hutely managed to answer my question and explain other preparations before our royal date. "Yes, Dan, they know who we are and where we're going. Like I said before, this is a very homogeneous society. Furthermore, supreme leaders are referred to as kings here, Danny boy. This is like Europe's feudal system during their Middle Ages around 1200 ACE. Whereas Europe had feudal castles, the Zhou had feudal walled cities. The term emperor starts with Fu Su's father, Qin Shi Huangdi, or first sovereign emperor. Before he gained power during the 'Warring States Period,' he was also known as King Zheng," Hutely said while unhooking himself from the oxcart.

"I bet you're glad to be free of that ritual, aye, Hutely," I said jokingly.

"Rituals are no joking matter here, Danny boy, they are the binding cultural glue. I was part of an ongoing ritual called 'scrub the barbarian before meeting royalty.' From the royal courtyard to peasant courtyard, the same rituals are performed."

"Absolutely, Hutely, but don't they have laws?" I asked, thinking of the American system back home. Hutely whinnied wearily and continued his ritual response.

"Rituals function as laws and are performed every day from sunrise to sundown. City dwellers and farmers look to the palace for divine inspiration, reassurance, and stability. If the palace skips a single synchronized ceremony, the consequences could be catastrophic. There are rite of passage, exercise, behavioral, astrological, matrimonial— numerically based—and birthing ritualistic ceremonies. I got a feeling we'll experience a serious ritual involving a turtle shell soon, Dan," Hutely concluded, moving slow while stretching his sore legs.

To my surprise, Shi and Teng came running up and hooked themselves to the oxcart and headed through a bronze gate leading into the industrial zone. "Okay," I said, "so how are we supposed to get around? More importantly, where did the missing mule go?" I asked, feeling left behind.

"He's over there," Fu Su and Chang answered quickly while pointing to an incredible bronze chariot with a royal teenager at the helm. Our eyes immediately met, and he smiled at me. Just barely still in my teens, the young driver looked to be my same age. Jumping off the chariot, he quickly hooked Hutely up to it and invited us to climb aboard.

"We mustn't keep Cheng or Hutely waiting. They just might take off without us," Chang said, grabbing Fu Su and I by the hand and pulling us toward the chariot. Once aboard, we were taken on a tour of the industrial zone for the benefit of the books.

"Welcome. My name is Song, and I was sent by my uncle to show you around."

"Thank you, King Cheng, my saddlebags and my fellow time travelers are honored by your presence. We look forward to your guidance, Song," said Hutely to his highness. Chang and Fu Su bowed and went on their knees and kissed his royal robe. This left me awkwardly standing by myself, waiting for a guidance song. Being a musician myself and an amateur singer-songwriter, I was anxious to hear the young driver belt one out. I missed his king title while being dragged to the chariot by Chang.

"So, Cheng," I said, "belt us out a good one!" Hutely turned his head and gave me a blank stare.

"He is Song, Dan!" Hutely belched out in an unbelieving tone.

"Okay... oh master music mule," I said. *"He is the song and writes the song that makes the whole city sing,"* I added melodically, which sent Chang and Fu Su rolling around the chariot floor laughing. "He's like an ancient Chinese Barry Manilow," I thought aloud.

King Cheng, or Song as his friends know him, was hip to the scene and belted out, *"We got to be ye... we got to be ye."*

After receiving a look of anticipation from Song, I took the second line. *"No matter how far, by chariot or car, I got to be me."* Song gave me a high-five, which fueled my origination theory once again.

"Ye refers to us as a whole, Dan, and King Cheng is also known as Song." With that said, we all had a good laugh. All of us except Hutely, that is. He was still reeling from his nightmare bath.

King Cheng started pointing out the different shops and explaining what each tradesman was working on. Our first shop stop was with a potter. It was clear that Song spent time around the industrial zone. He knew all the tradesmen on a first-name basis.

"Yandi is making a series of vessels for grain storage. Each side has two large decorative handles, and each vessel sits on a pedestal. After completion, each one is loaded on a cart and taken to another shop for bronzing or to be painted. Ones headed for the palace are usually adorned with a silk finish." Chang especially lit up when she spotted a lacquer-ware varnished alter piece. "They excite me too, Chang," Song said. "Yandi is also one heck of a wood carver and finisher." I found out later the varnish was extracted from the sap of sumac trees. Must have been a pre-Taoist-era chemist accomplishment, I suppose.

While watching Yandi work his magic, Chang told me how silk was discovered.

"Around 2,696 BCE, the goddess Leizu, the wife of Shangti, had a cocoon fall in her teacup. It unraveled and revealed a spectacular and continuous thread of silk," she said excitedly.

"Doesn't her husband Shangti have a Zhou Dynasty connection?" I asked.

"Yes, Dan," Chang agreed admiringly. "He is an ancestor of the Zhou royals. The heavenly couple realized the transformative quality of silk and planted rows of mulberry trees for silkworms to spin their thread." Once again, they must have been Taoist at heart.

"That makes sense, Chang," I said. "You might say that silk production symbolized the dynastic cycle of change exemplified by the fall of the Shang and rise of the Zhou."

"You might say that, but I feel the dynastic cycle is not so harmonious," Chang lamented, gaining the attention of Song. Song, or King Cheng, glanced a worried look our way, but he continued his touring duties.

Next, we visited another shop that resembled a paint studio. "You won't see many of these paintings in your time, Danny boy," Hutely whinnied. Chan, the shop foreman, had a beautiful display laid out for all to see. He bowed and knelt the entire time we were there.

"You may rise, Chan," said Song, but Chan continued to kneel the whole time. Hutely said there was something going on in the eastern lands and everyone here was careful to show their allegiance to the young king. Anyway, there were portraits of Cheng and his royal family that were placed in front of all the other paintings. Behind the royal display were nature scenes on pottery and ceramic jade pieces speckled the shop floor.

As Cheng walked with Fu Su and Chang, I stayed with Hutely close to the chariot. He told me that the Zhou made improvements on Shang artisanship. "You see, Dan, Zhou craftsman paid greater attention to detail and focused on aesthetics," said Hutely, admiring all the art pieces that were laid out.

"Absolutely, Hutely, just look at what great athletic shape Shi and Teng are in," I said, feeling a little out of shape.

"No... no... , Dan. aesthetics, not athletics! Remember when you said I needed a hearing aid... well?"

"Well... they kind of sound the same, Hutely!"

"Yes, they do, my boy, but they're different from homophones like *would* and *wood*. They sound the same. Aesthetics simply puts the emphasis on beauty and good taste!"

"Yeah, well, I guess things that taste good are beautiful to you, my friend. Even things that shouldn't taste good occupy your feed bag!"

"At least I'm not a picky eater like a certain human I know," said Hutely who had kept a keen eye out for more farm-cart droppings.

Hutely and I didn't realize that our tour friends had rejoined us and were standing by the chariot listening to our conversation. "What's all the yelling about?" Song inquired interrogatively. Chang and Fu Su were grinning because they had been around us enough to have witnessed firsthand our playful banter. King Cheng let out a luxurious laugh and motioned Hutely to go, but we didn't move an inch. It seems Chan, who had livestock of his own, was feeding Hutely a rice bowl. Still in a jovial mood, King Cheng, who was waiting to progress in two ways, patiently waited for Hutely to finish. While waiting, he went over to a bundle of bamboo strips that he seemed to read and interpret.

"What in the world is Song doing?" I asked.

"He's taking inventory," Fu Su answered quickly.

"With those bamboo strips?"

"Yes, he is," Fu Su said, taking out a small version of the bamboo bundle from his undergarment. "I use mine to calculate troop sizes, distances, and weapon stockpiles."

"Back in my time, we use calculators with buttons that represent numbers that you push."

"Song's commercial arithmetic bundle has a series of two digits, Dan. He can then do two- digit decimal multiplication," Fu Su added just before the tour commenced again. A smiling and bowing Chan retrieved the empty, licked-clean bowl, and soon we were on our way. Song looked satisfied with his stock count and took the helm of the chariot once again.

Our next stop was a metal shop. To our surprise, the place was packed with Song's royal subjects. There were potters, painters, bronze workers, farmers (including Shi and Teng) and the Duke of Zhou himself, the self-appointed regent of the Zhou Dynasty. The atmosphere seemed ripe for a ceremony. Chan had to stall us until the ceremony was ready for the teenager of the hour, Song.

The Duke of Zhou, who referred to himself as Uncle Dan, was obviously the best dressed person in the place. His outer robe and headdress were brown, purple, and green, but the colors changed shades as he walked. His inner layers were golden silk with white lapels that reached down to his ornamented, jeweled shoes. His royal guards surrounded him, signaling to everyone to kneel. Uncle Dan had Song stand by him in front of the shop as he addressed the crowd.

"We are here today to honor the remarkable ascendancy of my nephew, Cheng, from apprenticeship to master craftsman," said Uncle Dan, putting his arm around Song. "He is now the new supervisor of the storehouses." Uncle Dan paused as the crowd gave Song a rousing ovation but continued after the guards signaled everyone to be silent. "Despite his youthful age, he has amassed an impressive body of work. His skilled, script cast onto bronze ware and his revising of the lost wax method of production in the casting process has confounded and impressed his former Zhou superiors." Uncle Dan then made his way through the crowd and unveiled several bells, cauldrons, tripod pots, tureens with lids, and vases with lids that were Song's handiwork.

"Remember Yandi's remarkable grain vessel, Dan?" Hutely heehawed happily.

"Absolutely, Hutely, but now it has bronze inscriptions and, let's see, eleven characters."

"Very good, my boy," Hutely whinnied smiling. "This one, however, is a total Song creation from start to finish except for the inscription commemorating his new title. It will be one of the official grain storage pieces at the royal court," Hutely belched, beaming with pride for the young king. "The silk script casting is incredible," he concluded casually.

While we were discussing Song's amazing craftsmanship, his highness was thanking everyone for coming. As he thanked them all individually, he dismissed them and sent each back to work at their shops. I stayed with Song and met many of his adoring subjects. I had a few questions for the young king. Chang and Fu Su joined the Duke of Zhou in the chariot and Hutely pulled them toward the royal courtyard under heavy escort.

Song preferred to walk, so we both took the long way to the royal residence.

"If you don't mind me asking, Song, who's really in charge here?" I asked, sensing there was more going on here than meets the eye.

"Well, Dan, I'll tell you right off that I went through a king's coronation after my father, King Wu of Zhou, died." Song then started to tear up. "In reality... I'm a king in waiting. Uncle Dan wields supreme power, and I now run the royal storehouses," Song said with a slight hint of satisfaction. "My family is now divided because Uncle Dan claimed the regency and occupies my throne."

"Let me guess... you're too young, right?" I said, feeling a fellow teenager's pain.

"Yeah, something like that, Dan," Song said, but then he made me sit down and take a listen to what was really happening. "All this seemed to come about because of a planetary conjunction."

"A planetary, what?" I asked.

"Mercury, Venus, Mars, Jupiter, and Saturn came together in the northwestern sky above our people's land. We all knew the Shang's days were numbered. So my grandfather, King Wen, took it as a sign to make war on the Shang who used to rule over the Zhou."

"How come their days were numbered?"

"According to Uncle Dan, their leaders started thinking they were gods and lost focus on the people's needs, especially during monsoons and floods. This caused great suffering. The Zhou leaders saw through this false divinity claim and decided the Shang no longer had a mandate to rule from heaven."

"Back home in my country, the United States of America, our sixteenth president, Abraham Lincoln, felt that it's not whether God is on our side; rather, we need to be on God's side. At the time, he was fighting a bloody civil war!"

"Exactly, Dan!" Song said, bowing in agreement. "When you start thinking that you're 'holier than thou,'" he added, "you lose the grace once afforded to you." I could sense right away that Song had wisdom beyond his years. I also sensed he needed to get something off his chest, so I urged him to continue his story about his fractured family's feud.

"Please go on, Song, I would really like to know what's going on. I'd ask the all-knowing ass, but he took off with your uncle and everyone else," I said, which brought a smile to Song's face.

"After the Shang fell and my grandfather died, my father and his brothers threw off our Shang overlords. Suddenly, my people, the Zhou, were in charge. King Wu, my father, had to make quick decisions to establish what I call the 'Three T's,' which are trust, trade, and tranquility," Song said, obviously versed in governing.

"Sounds like a good recipe to fulfill a mandate from heaven," I said, still wondering what was wrong with his uncles.

"I suppose you're wondering about my uncles. At first everything was fine," he said, raising his arms in disgust. "The trouble started when my dad appointed the deposed Shang king's young son, Wu Geng, to oversee the newly acquired, rebellious Eastern Zhou territory. He sent my uncles, Guanshu Xian, Caishu Du, and Huoshu Chu, to oversee him and the conquered lands."

"Sounds like you guys were kind of in the same junk."

"Like me, Uncle Dan thought he was too young to rule. So then…" Tears streamed down Song's cheeks. "Dad died," Song exclaimed, trying desperately to conceal his tears. I offered my condolences and thought he might want to be alone, but he called me back.

"You need a minute?" I asked him gently. Smiling, he squeezed my hand and continued his explanation.

"Before he died, my dad gave Uncle Dan and Uncle Shi the royal chancellorship and protectorate in the West. Uncle Dan claimed the regency and he took over the court. He and Uncle Shi became all powerful. Word reached my uncles in the East, and they rebelled and joined local Shang loyalists against us here in Fenghao."

"Now I get it," I said, shaking my head.

"My uncles in the East accused Uncle Dan of usurpation of the throne. But everyone in the Western Zhou accepted it after the initial shock wore off."

"How do you feel about not being king?" I asked him.

"If you knew the Duke of Zhou, Uncle Dan, you would want him in charge!"

"Isn't he the author of the I Ching, or the Book of Changes?"

"I think that's what they're called," Song said, shrugging his shoulders. "He's written so much. I've only been able to read a fraction of his writings," Song said with a hint of exhaustion.

"That's a big reason we're here, Song," I said. "Believe it or not, Hutely's saddlebags are full of these 'Civilizing Books' that a future emperor tried to destroy. Their covers are made of dragon skin and the characters will only reappear if we travel to that period they were written in," I said, trying my best to explain our mission.

"I see," Song said, "But what's this? Our Jade Emperor extols good fortune here!"

"I'm talking about an earthbound emperor who extols hardship and rules over kings, but his earthly title won't exist until around 200 BCE. Fortunately, the Zhou Dynasty and the Duke of Zhou will provide a blueprint for sages and future dynasties to come," I said, stressing that a ruthless future leader wants to erase Uncle Dan's incredible literary teachings. I explained to Song what Hutely, Chang, Fu Su, and I saw firsthand regarding his Legalist cruelty. Song got it, and we headed in the direction of the royal compound.

I could see the colorful architecture rising above the walls that surrounded the royal compound. Unlike the peasant homes or even the upper-class homes that had three connecting wings called bags, the royal roofs were brightly colored. The temple, palace, and inner and outer courtyard roofs had impressive yellow glazed tiles that gave off a blinding sheen. Song said they used green vermilion paint for the supporting pillars of the temple and the palace. I had to take his word for it on that one. Before entering the royal residence, Song had gates he wanted to show me first.

"Before we go in, Dan, I want to show you some bronze work I helped create." We then walked to the east gate of the royal compound that was in the form of a dragon. "Our gates represent the four directions," he said, sounding like a tour guide again. "This dragon is called Ao Kuang and represents the east." Song went on to show me three more gates. "Each one also represents a season of the year," he added enthusiastically. The west gate was called Ao Jun, the north was Ao Shun, and the south gate was called Ao K'in.

"They look like variations of the Jade Dragon we saw wrapped around the magic ferry!" I shouted, separating my arms wide to relate how big the Jade Dragon was. "She is mother to the dragon-skinned books in Hutely's saddlebags."

"Magic ferry? Hutely's saddlebags... ? Anyway," he said, scratching his head. "A king chooses a dragon as a symbol of his kingdom. Each dragon symbolizes good luck and power to summon rain during droughts and strength during other seasonal challenges," said Song with a perplexed look on his face.

"Hutely says kings realize what season their dynasty is in. By season, I mean, whether good or tough times are going to happen. You know, patterns in people's relationships over time... securing life's partners," I said, not realizing we were being surrounded. This included Hutely who had two teenage couples on his back. There were around ten couples in all. Each couple bowed before King Cheng and formed what looked like a choir's loft on a rectangular raised patio outside the southern gate. Hutely, Song, the books, and I took a listen.

Aren't we stuck in patterns. Where's the appreciation?
The lost song runs rampant, unchained mixing with the atoms.

Isn't the mind thinking everything, not a tunnel seeking the light?
The light is our gift in our smiles, fears, and sight.
If I believe, does it make us free?
If we love, does it have to be proven or defined?
Aren't we stuck in patterns, where's the initiation?
Is it a mass migration of love sweeping our generation?
Isn't the mind thinking everything, not a tunnel seeking the light?
The light is our gift in our smiles, fears, and sight.

I must say that the young couples chorus impressed me. After they finished singing, each couple presented Song with a ceremonial reed with a silk bow attached to it. Hutely said the teenagers wanted to show solidarity with the young king. The selection was titled "Patterns," with each couple adding a lyric to the composition. They had petitioned the Duke of Zhou to let them perform for the young king as Hutely looked on. Hutely then took the traveling troupe to where we were.

"Shouldn't that song be called 'Questions,' Hutely?"

"Maybe, Danny boy, but these young people are students studying their history. Starting with the fabled Xian Dynasty through the Shang, they see patterns that concern them."

"Well, they and King Cheng are the future, aye, Hutely?"

"Yes, they are," Hutely agreed while looking for something to graze on. Not finding anything, Hutely explained our current situation and what was next. "The Duke of Zhou, even though he is in charge, needs his nephew's approval to put down his brothers' betrayal in the East. Fu Su is advising Uncle Dan on military matters while Chang prepares an augury ceremony for Song," said Hutely, chewing on finally found fresh flowers.

"Song told me about his uncles, but you lost me about Chang's ceremony! Are we drilling holes for any particular reason?" I asked, wondering how Song got so versed in the trades.

"Not auger, Dan, remember muscle-power technology and that you are from the future. Ancient tortoise shells are used to determine future outcomes. An augury is a sign like an omen of things to come!"

"Absolutely, Hutely, that's why that number should have been called 'Questions'!"

"Okay, Dan, and yes, auguries are used to answer pressing questions. Either one works for me. Let me clarify if that's okay with you?"

"Absolutely, Hutely! Do tell."

"Auguries, or omens, are used to interpret and solve common issues currently under suspicion and in need of further examination. One wants answers to see patterns and verify solutions concerning questions they may have," said Hutely who was packing in words like Bob Dylan, a little, but not that much, but still, tight. He continued with an emphasis on patterns. "You see, Dan, patterns comprise a well-thought-out individual movement."

"Absolutely, Hutely of the long sentence," I said, feeling I've finally got him! Then I heard him refer to the "Tube of time." To begin with, and according to Hutely, we are the tube hurling through time. Our tubular being extends through space. Cut it in half and one can see the identifying relationships and connections. You guessed it, "Patterns!" Hutely, the analytical animal, was making sense out of the young couple's composition.

"So you see, my boy, to appreciate a dynastic place in time, you must initiate a cutting of the tube." Easier said than done, I thought as I remembered a more tangible tool for answering questions that Hutely spoke of.

"Absolutely, Hutely, but let's slow things down a bit. How can anyone answer questions regarding the future using a tortoise shell?"

"I'll show you how," said Song after thanking Hutely for his extended explanation.

Chapter 7

· · · · · · · · · · · ·

The I CHING and the Tortoise Shells

The books in the saddlebags were "Rumbling bumbling, stumbling" as we made our way into the royal compound through the south gate. You would have thought they had ESPN or something. Their movements while taking dictation started to tickle Hutely. He tried hard to hold back his laughter but failed. His busted chainsaw screeched in all its vulgar rudeness. Five astute, yet alarmed, teenagers wedged pillows between Hutely and the saddlebags, thus, putting an end to his high-pitched hysteria.

The Duke of Zhou came running up and directed the youthful choir to the southern outer quarters of the compound that was designated for kids, young adults, and servants. Only adults were allowed to travel freely in the royal compound. Song, of course, was the exception to the rule. Fu Su and Chang were honored guests and got a free pass. Because I was with Hutely, I too was given roaming rights. At least that's what Hutely told me as Uncle Dan was shooing the youngsters away.

All along the rectangle-shaped royal compound walls were young mulberry trees. The whole city can be described as rectangles within rectangles with the outermost rectangle (outside the city walls) being farm fields and burial sites. Sumac trees separated various parts of the royal compound, however. The ceremonial altar was outside and north of the Dougong or bracket-style roofed palace, but it was south of the temple that had a similar design. Our first stop was the royal palace.

In the middle of the palace was an incredible atrium covered with a latticework of fauna. It ran north and south, weaving through walkways leading to different rooms. These were the royals' quarters and where

Song grew up. Everything that wasn't growing was painted gold, yellow, or red. Silk rugs led to all the royal rooms. Royal portraits lined the walls. Each royal had their portrait hanging conspicuously next to their door. Before entering, we were fitted with gold slippers to wear while walking through the palace. They even had four golden donkey-hoof coverings for pleasant smelling Hutely. Everything was impeccably clean.

The atrium had an incredible bamboo bridge that was over a pond filled with colorful gold, orange-white, and red koi fish. Hutely said, "Those making it to the top of a waterfall turned into beautiful flying golden dragons." There were birds walking around us and floating on the pond. In the water were mandarin ducks whose orange, red, gray, and blue-green head stripes were impressive. Cranes walked in and around pine trees that grew around the pond. Brown-eared pheasants also inhabited the atrium.

Bamboo benches surrounded the pond with a red lacquer-finished pavilion overhead. Fu Su, Chang, Hutely, and I sat on the benches and waited for Uncle Dan and Song who had retired to their rooms to return. However, sleep overtook us and even Hutely sacked out on a bench. The saddlebags were still as well.

The most tranquil chimes sounded, signaling to servants to feed the guests. We awoke to rice bowls and hot tea. A feed bag was strapped on Hutely's muzzle, but instead of tea when finished eating, he drank from the pond. Red gowned women bowed to us as we ate and cleared away our dishes when we were finished. They led us to the north entrance of the palace where orange outfitted manservants gave us back our original footwear.

From the north entrance of the palace, we beheld the splendid altar. It was bronze plated in the shape of a long dragon. It had a line of characters that were inscribed in silk across its body. Hutely translated it to mean, "Sons of Heaven." A silk-inscribed man was riding the dragon. There were characters inscribed above him that read, "To the heavens for peace." This is where Song was to consult the tortoise shells. This would determine whether to quell the "Rebellion of the Three Guards," which of course referred to Uncle Dan's brothers and Song's uncles. Below the dragon's clawed feet were five smoldering cauldrons. In each one was a tortoise shell with questions written on them.

There were five rows of benches in front of the altar. The servants instructed us to sit and observe. From behind the altar, King Cheng, the Duke of Zhou, and the Duke of Shao, or Shi, half-brother to Uncle Dan, came out and knelt before the cauldrons. They would later be known as the "Ruling Triumvirate." Uncle Dan raised up the tortoise shells one by one, revealing charred characters and cracks on each shell. Song had written out questions, and now he was interpreting the scorched answers. His uncles were advising him on what the heated cracks on the tortoise shells meant. The answers would not only indicate the fate of the rebellion, but also the fate of his uncle's siding with the Shang loyalists. "What do the shells say?" I said, looking to Hutely for answers.

"Patience," said Hutely in a faint voice.

"Surely your supersonic hearing must be able to hear what's being said." I started getting please-be-quiet looks from Fu Su and Chang. Chang then took my hand and led me to the back-row benches to have a word with me.

"This is a sacred ceremony, Dan, and it takes time," she whispered faintly. "People's futures and the course of history is at stake." With that said, we both resumed our places in the front.

"Song may need some teenage companionship after what's foretold here, Dan," said Hutely softly. "So please stop fidgeting and sit still. Hey, try daydreaming. You're quite good at that," he added while keeping an eye on the proceedings.

"Absolutely, Hutely," I said, but too concerned about Song's frame of mind to react to Hutely's wisecrack. Song was a talented kid who had the weight of the world on his shoulders. After a couple of hours, the Duke of Zhou lowered the five tortoise shells back in the cauldrons. A quick clap of his hands ended the ritual. The Duke of Zhou and his brother walked into the temple without a word.

Song remained kneeling for a second and hung his head. We all sat there breathlessly until he got up and walked to where I was sitting. He looked at me displaying a firm resolve, but then hung his head again. This time I knew he didn't need a moment. By the expression on his face, I could almost guess what the shells revealed. I asked anyway. "So, ah, what's the verdict?"

"We must put down the rebellion and my uncles must be punished," he said, looking up to the heavens.

"Hope not too severely," I said, not wanting to be unsympathetic.

"Their punishment will match their betrayal!" Hutely sensed the young king's anger and nudged both of us to follow Chang and Fu Su into the temple.

Entering the temple, you could feel the presence of royal Zhou ancestors. All my senses were tingling, and Hutely's tail and mane stood straight up but quickly fell back down. There were shrines to the Sons of Heaven. Paintings of past and present Zhou royalty hung on all four walls. Intertwined between the royals were hangings of bronze silk-inscribed dragons and deities. I saw impressive wood carvings of Tu Ti, Shangti, and his wife Leizu.

Ceremonial vases on pedestals filled with grain, rice, and millet also lined the walls. Large cauldrons were lit, providing light and shadows to celebrate the living and the dead. Silk rugs were strewn about the floor for temple goers to meditate and pray. Chairs hadn't started their supporting role yet in temples, only thrones existed and were only for royal bottoms. Suddenly the cauldrons were snuffed out, and the room went pitch black. I managed to hold on to Hutely's tail with one hand and Fu Su's coat with the other.

Out of the darkness arose an octagonal image from behind a glowing green ceremonial altar on the north wall. It was composed of eight red and white trigrams with a circular, spiraling multicolored Yin and Yang symbol in the middle. Its light revealed many robed figures seated and meditating on some of the silk rugs. "Hey, Hutely..."

"Hay! Where?" yelled Hutely, forgetting where he was for a moment. All eyes were suddenly on the master mule. Embarrassed, but also disappointed there was no hay to eat, Hutely smiled and gave them all the hooves-up signal. All eyes then turned to three golden thrones in front of the green altar. "Don't do that again, Dan," said Hutely, whispering as he looked for a place to set his hairy carcass down.

"I just wanted you to know that there's a large dog bed behind you, Hutely."

"Thanks, Danny boy," he said, while making himself at home on the overgrown cushion. I took my place on the floor as well to avoid drawing any more attention. All the robed royals continued their silent meditation.

Hutely started explaining the impressive detailed image. "You see, Dan, each trigram is arranged across from its opposite. Heaven is opposite earth, water is opposite fire, wind is across from thunder, and mountain is opposed to lake. That large octagon, taken as a whole, is commonly known as bagua around here."

"Absolutely, Hutely, Yin and Yang control the opposites since they're in the center," I said, not knowing really what that meant. The group meditation continued with Uncle Dan, Song, and his half-uncle nowhere in sight.

"Well, Dan, you make up one half," said Hutely. "You are bright, positive, masculine or male, so you are Yang." Did Hutely just pay me a compliment? "On the other hand, Chang is Yin and represents negative, dark, and mysterious femininity. The Yin and Yang interaction influences the destinies of creatures, including me, and other worldly outcomes." Upon hearing the conversation between Hutely and me, Chang maneuvered her rug close to mine. This moving around on rugs reminded me of a restless kindergarten nap-time session when I was a kid.

"Don't let it go to your head, Dan," Chang said, wanting to explain things. "As a female, remember, we give birth. We may seem negative, but it's only because we're extra cautious due to all the responsibility placed upon us women."

"Well said," said a whispering Hutely, "but..."

"I'm not finished, Hutely," she said, gripping Hutely's mane. "Our wombs are dark, but life comes through us. The deep forest is dark, but its trees give off life-sustaining oxygen. As you were saying, Hutely?"

"All good points, princess, but earth, *di*, makes up the lower two lines of the hexagram. Humankind, *ren*, occupies the two middle lines and heaven, *tian*, makes up the top two. The two trigrams that make up a hexagram demonstrate the multiple ways Yin and Yang interact and transform each other. But not just each other, it demonstrates the codependence between the natural domain, *tian* and *di*, and the human domain, *ren*. Finally, the Book of Changes is the oldest system of investigation into the nature of relationships. Its randomness is like quantum physics in your time, Dan."

"Absolutely, Hutely, but you went over my head a few sentences ago," I said bedazzled, but remembering a not-so-pleasant memory. "I do seem to recall the founder of quantum physics whose name was Max Planck. I learned something about him in my chemistry class," I said, scratching my head nervously. "Now, let's see. He said hot objects don't radiate energies in a consistent fashion that exist on the sub-atomic plane."

"Wow, Dan, you'll make a fine Taoist," Chang said, patting me on the back.

"Uh, not really," I moaned in response. "I failed chemistry in high school because Mr. Van Trout thought I cheated on the final exam off my jelly pastry while I was eating it."

"How does one cheat off food? Are the answers baked into every bite?" Chang chided Van Trout's determination. "It sounds fishy to me," she added.

"It wasn't your fault, Dan," Hutely insisted. "You crammed all night for that test, and you didn't stop to eat until it was time for testing."

"Absolutely, Hutely, I picked up a couple of jelly donuts on my way to class," I replied, wondering how Hutely knew that. "Starving, and unable to concentrate, I scarfed them down while taking the test."

"Well, I hope he had the courtesy to wait till you were finished eating before he grabbed the test and failed you!" Chang answered angrily. "What a crumb, aye, Hutely!"

"Where?" said Hutely, scouring the floor.

"That's just it... he said nothing until he handed back the graded tests the next day!" Once again, the meditating royals shushed us. "By then, I had long since thrown my napkins away, and of course, the donuts had been eaten. All the evidence that could clear my name was gone," I whispered, trying not to make any more of a scene.

"Anyway, Dan, you were quite correct about Max Planck," Hutely said, giving me a glazed look after thinking about donuts. "Think of the smallest amount, quanta, of energy released or taken in. Each sub-atomic unit is unique, let's say like you and Chang compared to the immense world. However, your reaction to stimulus, though unique, when combined, quantum, affects the surrounding environment in varying degrees."

"Absolutely, Hutely, so the study of thermodynamics led to the discovery of electromagnetic radiant interactions known as quantum actions," I said, which gave me a thermodynamic headache. With too much said, Uncle Dan, Song, and Half-Uncle Shi entered and sat on their royal thrones. The Duke of Zhou addressed us, the servants, and the kneeling temple royalty.

"In my contemplation, I try to see all things as part of a great whole. This way, I can determine the actual meaning of life," said the Duke of Zhou, raising his arms in the air and gesturing to the four directions. "Changes require investigations into the nature of the universe," he added, bringing his hands together in prayer. "The best person is like water which benefits all and doesn't compete with others," he said, turning his attention to the young king. "Advancement shines on you and your industrious work performed. Your promotion, Song, will be and has been well executed," Uncle Dan said, putting his hand on Song's shoulder. "We must adapt knowing when to act in the main stream of time."

"This sounds like a call to war, Hutely, if I'm not mistaken," I said with a hint of anxiety. Hutely sighed and gave me one of those "There's more here than meets the eye" looks. The Duke of Zhou continued his justification lecture.

"The creative and mindful leader from the beginning directs activities from behind the scenes." As I stated before, with the idea of homogeneity, everyone knows anyway. "This is to ensure that those sharing power share his enthusiasm. He needs dedicated support to pursue worthwhile goals." Having turned his gaze on the attentive audience, Uncle Dan again turned to Song, putting both hands on the young king's shoulders while speaking reassuringly. "Despite difficulties you may face, appropriate behavior sends you successfully on your way. You must remember, nephew, sovereignty is both a curse and a blessing full of pride, greed, and immodesty. The temptation we face in the East is to ignore it and let it develop naturally. If we do nothing, a doable solution may turn into a sizable problem."

Having heard the duke's words, I realized Hutely might be facing a sizable problem of his own. His body was violently shaking all over. Freaking out, I grabbed his mane to see what the matter was. Hutely turned to me nonchalantly and said, "Relax, Danny boy, the books once again are taking dictation. Their agitation reveals earth-shaking ideas with hyperbole intensity," he whinnied while whisking up rice pudding he got from a sympathetic servant.

"Absolutely, Hutely, they must be recording the 'Book of Changes,' or at least part of it."

"That's right, Dan," he said, hoof-pumping the attentive servant who solved his latest hunger crisis. All of us knew there was another crisis that needed immediate attention. Of course, with crisis comes opportunity. The "Ruling Triumvirate" needed to resist apathetic temptation and secure the foundations of Confucianism by putting down the "Rebellion of the Three Guards."

It was hard saying goodbye to the Duke of Zhou, Shi, and especially Song who I had formed a bond of friendship with. Oh, and of course all the smiling servants and citizens who were instrumental in making our visit a success. Hutely, the books, Chang, Fu Su, and I left the temple, found our oxcart, and headed out of town toward the river.

Chapter 8

· · · · · · · · · · · ·

The Just Cause for Educated Gentlemen
(Play in the Sand)

We approached the red pentagon-shaped ferry without the usual security precaution. The golden pulsating fenced cage must have been turned off. Chu Yuan, in all his royal garb, welcomed us and told us to watch our step while boarding. His hands were firmly on the rudder and the sword. We all floated over the rice floor and sat on the bright yellow benches. He spoke as the black water began rippling and bubbling below.

"The just cause for educated gentleman needs strategic alliances to keep up the good fight despite dangerous warring factions. If one is to play in the sand, the unjust rebellion must be quashed first," said Chu Yuan with a slight smirk separating his black beard. The Jade Dragon rose out of the turbulent black water. Its wicked, yet benevolent gaze fixated on Hutely's saddlebags. Like baby chicks to its mother, the books hungered for reunion, but it wasn't time yet.

The magic ferry once again splashed down on an underground river, which turned into a green glowing well. The cylindrical well was a familiar sight. Unfamiliar to us, except for Hutely of course, was the face of a new passenger on the ferry. Hutely smiled at and addressed the stranger dressed in peasant rags. "Nice to see you, Fenhua, and as usual, you have perfect time-traveling sense." The name Fenhua means youthful action.

"Likewise, Master Hutely, always an honor to serve for the good of the people." The dragon-skinned books shook at the sound of his voice. Fenhua looked to be my age with a youthful, energetic gaze as he greeted us. "I will be your guide through the next phase of your journey after the picture show," he said, bowing in each of our directions. We all bowed back and smiled cautiously at our assigned traveling companion. Once again Tu Ti appeared out of nowhere. He greeted us warmly, rose, and started the 360-degree round theater in motion. He narrated events as they passed before our eyes.

"Because of the usurpation, large strips of the Eastern Zhou's empire rebelled against the government at Fenghao. It was Guanshu and Caishu who instigated the rebellion by convincing young Wu Geng to go against the Western Zhou." All three appeared on the screen in a palace room as if zoomed in on. Tu Ti continued his narration. "The brothers bullied the young leader to call for insurgency. A third brother entered and suffered the same fate."

"I don't think Huoshu wanted to join his brothers, Hutely," I said sympathetically.

"By the initial expression on his face, maybe not. But remember, Danny boy, there was delayed communication between the Duke of Zhou and his brothers. It took sixty days to get a message through to the East by land. Look at all those passes and routes heading east. They had over a year of self-rule." The theater showed a panorama of the Zhou Dynasty, which demonstrated the point beautifully.

"Absolutely, Hutely, look at the rebel state of Ying. The Ying River Valley connects with the Luoyang plain and joins Nanyang Basin. It's a long way to travel!"

"Not to mention rebel control of eastern roads, and especially the ones leading to the middle Yangtze region," Fu Su added from a military man's point of view. "They've left farm fields and crops unguarded, which will cost them dearly. Well-fed soldiers controlling the food supply tend to fight better," he added, speaking from experience.

"The Dongyi polities of Shandong promoted the rebellious insurrection. But why the Huai River region? They weren't affiliated with either the Shang or the Zhou, but over time were turned to rebel," Chang said, raising her arms in the air.

"Are you all quite finished?" Tu Ti inquired with a slight hint of irritation.

"Oh... yes, sorry, Tu Ti," I said. The theater pictures were revealing and comparable to Google Maps, according to Hutely, so we couldn't resist interpreting them. We could see the loyal Zhou positions that were still intact after a year of ineffective attacks by Shang rebels.

"Right!" Tu Ti replied energetically. "High Fenhau, how are you?" he added, but then resumed narrating. "King Cheng, the Duke of Zhou, and Shi led a second attack along with a military strategist, Lu Shang. Eastern rebels were complacent, disorganized, and one pocket of resistance after another was wiped out by Zhou forces under the 'Triumvirate's command,'" Tu Ti exclaimed, resembling a lava lamp on steroids. "The second year of fighting saw the destruction of Yin and the death of Wu Geng."

"Unlike Song, Wu Geng didn't have the experiential wisdom to say no to an ill-advised civil war," said Fu Su, giving Chang a spirited hug. "Poor kid. It cost him and others their lives," he added somberly. Hutely was quick to spot the three brothers that caused his downfall.

"There's Caishu stealing a horse and chariot to escape the debacle," Hutely heehawed as Caishu high-tailed it. Fenhua shook his head and smiled but continued to remain silent.

"Absolutely, Hutely! I see him. But wasn't he banished or exiled?" I asked, trying to get my facts straight.

"Looks like he's banishing himself into a permanent exile," Chang said, shaking her head in disgust.

"Not the actions of a noble who sought the throne," Fu Su commented while observing the fate of Song's other turncoat uncles.

Tu Ti's light display kept us focused on major events as they happened. After the Three Guard's main force was defeated, Guanshu was executed while Huoshu was reduced in rank. By year's end, the cities of Feng and Pugu were under loyalist control.

The third year brought an end to the civil war, moreover, the "Rebellion of the Three Guards." King Cheng and the Duke of Zhou punished the Huai's fateful decision by capturing the city of Yan and expanding Zhou rule throughout the eastern seaboard. Relatives of the royal family were given important fief positions along the Yellow River and Taihang Mountains. To the contrary, Shang leaders were scattered among geographically unimportant areas on the fringes of the empire. With hostilities over, it was time to play in the sand.

Like the old bouncing ball sing-along when I was a kid, lyrics appeared and were sung by an incredible vocalist with a music accompaniment. The vocalist was none other than Fenhua. It swirled around our heads. Of course, the ball had a Yin and Yang symbol on it. The books began to jiggle, Hutely began to giggle, with the rest of us swaying to the inspiring tune. We all tried to harmonize as we sang along.

> *Play in the sand, if not for me than for yourself.*
> *Though you feel like sleeping, it could rain at any time.*
> *I'm feeling so alive, emotion lights my way.*
> *I'm feeling so defined, a glossary in a day...*
> *Your time is in demand, if not from me than for yourself.*
> *Run through a grass field, it could burn tomorrow.*
> *I'm feeling so alive, emotion lights my way.*
> *I'm feeling so defined, a glossary in a day...*
> *I have to go now, don't forget a word I've said.*
> *'Cause when we're dreaming, thoughts begin to fill our heads.*
> *We're feeling so alive, emotions light our way.*
> *We're feeling so defined, we're glossaries in a day...*

Suddenly the circular screen went blank. The Jade Dragon and Chu Yuan once again flew up the well. Before his ascension, Chu Yuan seemed to repeat himself when he said, "The just cause for educated gentlemen needs strategic alliances to keep up the good fight despite dangerous warring factions."

"Oh my god, Hutely, is this 'Groundhog Day'? or something. Do we have to relive the rebellion? Do the books need a refresher course?" Fenhua steadied the alarmed books that had begun to spasm inside their saddlebag chasm fearing a delayed reunion with mother dragon.

Tu Ti let out a hardy laugh, obviously having seen the movie; he saw it twice. "It's nice to laugh when there is so much sorrow in the underworld and above," Tu Ti related radiating joyous, yet tempered earth tones. He motioned us off the ferry and into the mist once again. Chang enjoyed the Taoist light display but looked to Fu Su for clarification on the Confucian-inspired quote and lyrical theme. Tu Ti bade us well as all of us exited the ferry with Hutely waltzing the plank.

"Is that the only dance he knows?" I said, trying to get around Hutely's expanded girth, and I don't mean saddlebags. I did have questions about who exactly was supposed to play in the sand.

"He's a big Strauss fan, you know," said Fenhua, "especially after we spent time in the Vienna Wood," he added. Hutely just smiled and started his latest history lesson.

"You see, Dan," said the waltzing Mule-Tilda. "At first the feudal system had good government like in the state of Lu where the Duke of Zhou set up shop. He appointed competent men to various positions, and they weren't always relatives. If a son of royalty was deemed worthy, he still had to have the king's blessing."

"Absolutely, Hutely, Uncle Dan had nothing but praise for Song's industrial abilities."

"Quite true, my boy. Cheng became a powerful king, and he saw his superior qualities in all his future appointees. In other words, powerful kings chose capable ministers to conduct the fief's business by first performing royal rituals with adherence to laws second."

"Absolutely, Hutely, of course a good leader leads by example and expects his appointees to do the same," I said, still wondering about the song while looking for sand.

"Appointees, my boy, is the key word here," Hutely whinnied, looking for a snack. "You see, Dan, fiefs weren't initially hereditary, but like I said before, kings surrounded themselves with skilled, moral ministers. If a royal was unfit to lead, a qualified appointee was chosen to take his place. An appointee resume would soon include a high score on a Confucian-style examination-system test." Hutely went on to say that Confucius thought people should think for themselves, and he demanded that of them. Furthermore, that ceremony and ritual encouraged internal compliance while laws, which were external, needed coercion. This made sense to me after seeing the ferocity of legalist law.

Chapter 9

· · · · · · · · · · · ·

Confucian Sons of Royal Concubines

As the mist cleared, Hutely was still dancing and nudging me with his snout to keep moving down the wooded path. Chang and Fu Su were arm-in-arm up ahead of us enjoying a couple's cuddle. Fenhua took the lead making sure we didn't get sidetracked. The wooded path soon opened into a huge clearing full of revelers dancing, singing, and taking part in activities resembling a medieval fair. Multicolored open-ended tents sprinkled the clearing like merchant kiosks you would find in a hippie mall.

"I feel like I'm back at Woodstock, Hutely," I said, noticing that Fenhua was communing and greeting young men dressed just like him.

"You never made it there, Danny boy," Hutely wearily whinnied while looking famished as usual. "You were about nine and totally engrossed in little league baseball."

"Absolutely, Hutely, but I was also over a thousand miles away and hadn't gotten my license yet."

"You were too young, and your cars wouldn't have made it anyway, my boy."

"Absolutely not, Hutely, they served me well and were good vehicles," I said, waiting for Hutely's condescending car critique.

"Let's see," Hutely pondered. "The Mustang made it a hundred feet, died, and was stolen by a motorcycle gang out of your friend's brother-in-law's shop. Your yellow duster was more a rusty red, and the back axle fell off while you were driving it. The Ford Fairlane's seats broke, and the engine quit. Turns out, the previous owner loved driving up the dunes and rolling back down them," said Hutely while

65

swatting me with his tail. "Oh yes, of course, the Maverick!" It was quite apparent Hutely was enjoying himself. Me, on the other hand, not so much.

"Ouch," I said. "Okay, Hutely, you're right. They were all lemons," I said as Fenhua directed us to a stage where puppeteers began a production for our benefit and a growing crowd that sat beside and around us. Fenhua joined them on stage and narrated a Confucian play that would claim its place in the Book of Documents. I opened up Hutely's saddlebags, where I noticed all six books were like idling lawnmowers, ready to cut, capture, and record the final grasslands of knowledge the H. G. Academy sent us to protect. At Hutely's request, I left the flaps open to allow the books more freedom of movement to sample the fair's wares.

"At the tender and impressionable age of sixteen, Confucius befriended a growing class of the 'impoverished, depressed, descendants of nobility.'" The puppets depicting Confucius and the descendants were dressed like Fenhua and his mates. According to Hutely, who had found an abandoned rice bowl, the growing class of descendants were the result of royal concubines that had become common at royal courts over the previous decades. Their sons, although royal, were shunned and denied titles. They became an intervening class with ties to the common folk's travails and to the educated elite who taught them how to stage successful protests. The saddlebag books were silently vibrating and taking in all the fair had to offer. To the contrary, Hutely's loud eating soon garnered more attention than the play.

"Quiet down, you're not in Japan, Hutely," I said.

"Sorry, Dan, it was just so tasty."

"Hutely, you ate the bowl! It sounded like you were eating someone's patio," I added, but quickly lowered my voice.

"It was biodegradable," he said in a defensive tone.

"In ten thousand years, maybe… ," I answered sarcastically. Fenhua narrated on after shushing me and apologizing for his ass's rude behavior. Embarrassed, you bet.

"Scene 1. A local duke of a small neighboring state was lamenting his ineffective court. He was tired of his incompetent relatives who, over the years, inherited their royal positions instead of earning them through knowledge and honorable deeds. He sought out the enlightened descendants. As former knights, Confucius included, they were schooled in the pious ways of the Duke of Zhou and early Zhou standards of excellence."

"Look, Hutely, that puppet reminds me of Song."

"The puppet to his left looks a lot like the Duke of Zhou," Hutely whinnied quietly.

"Scene 2," said Fenhua, giving us a concerned look. "The fed-up local duke appointed several outstanding, intervening descendants as officers and fired his unqualified greedy relatives," Fenhua said triumphantly. However, at this point, the puppets clashed. The duke and his new courtiers were executed by the duke's relatives; thus, custom and privilege was restored. "Confucius was appalled by this," said a visibly frustrated Fenhua. "As a result of this injustice, Confucius dedicated his life promoting education and ethical governance to make life better for the masses. Scene 3. Confucius founded a school dedicated to higher education. Behold the parade of puppets! They're students without regard for social status yet entering and leaving as fine gentlemen with moral conviction. Ability to pay was not a priority, and all are accepted freely!" Fenhau concluded gleefully. Hutely said Confucius achieved only lower-level government posts, but his best work was as a teacher.

After the puppet show, I couldn't help but wonder and think out loud, "Where was Confucius? Is there more to his story? Furthermore, where was Lao Tzu for that matter?" Hutely went on to explain that it was 531 BCE, and Confucius had died twenty years earlier. Lao Tzu was to pass this very day. To my surprise, and Chang's surprise, Fu Su overheard me and supplied the answers to my questions.

"Well, Dan," he said, "military officers had once been a positive force in protecting the people, road making, and food distribution. In other words, they were there for the people. This was especially true in the Kong lineage who were the direct ancestors of Confucius. His people were originally knights. Because of decentralization the Spring and Autumn period, characterized by Song and the Duke of Zhou, gave way to the brutal Warring States Period. My father triumphed and formed the Qin Dynasty. Unfortunately, he perverted both Confucianism and Taoism and established a cruel Legalist state."

"Back home in my country," I said, "we tried decentralization with the Articles of Confederation at first, but soon we realized it was too weak. Instead, we established a strong unified federal government. Although, we still fought a civil war a brief time in the future."

"The United States, as you know, did have a rebirth of freedom, Danny boy. The Han Dynasty will rise from the carnage and destruction wrought by the Qin Dynasty and take Chinese culture to new heights. The Han supplied the remembrance paper to the books in my saddlebags to preserve the Confucian Classics. While we were discussing, Fenhau and his royal descendants cleared the stage revealing a very large sandbox. Dozens of Fenhau's brethren had built connecting sand buildings resembling the Duke of Zhou's kingdom.

"Look, Hutely, they're playing in the sand!"

"They're not doing it for themselves, Dan. But just look at them. They're feeling so alive."

"Just a wee-bit overbearing," said Chang, giving Fu Su a defiant look.

"Absolutely, Hutely! They're glossaries in a day." The song finally made sense to me. Rain and fire were metaphors for dynastic rebellion and reform.

"Yes, they are, my boy. But are the Confucianist rebels or reformers?" It's remarkable how Hutely reads my thoughts. How could he have known what I was thinking?

"The Confucianist interventions are done by a relatively small group of reformers who have sincere, good intentions," Chang replied. "I'll give them that. However, being a Taoist, I, and those like me, focus on everyday life. We don't dwell on rigid societal, wishful change." Suddenly out of the nature or eastern forest appeared a procession led by Kwan Yin. She resembled a white, yellow, orange, and red lotus sunrise. All around her were babies and smiling woman wearing red and gold gowns. Each woman and child pair rode in on a big beautiful black, orange, and white tiger's back. The women had their shiny black hair up in buns while the little ones had silk headdresses on. They were the same tigers that rescued the books out of the fire. Hutely's saddlebag books continued their character-revealing ways.

Chang and Kwan Yin embraced a second time. To Chang, Kwan Yin was a life-giving sun that could never be extinguished. After greeting all the women and their babies, Chang elicited their help to sing the Taoist perspective. They ascended on top of a massive lotus flower like a heavenly chorus in the sky. This had a hypnotic effect on everyone at the fair.

It's hard to achieve independence when ensnared by things.
Inflexible master's code, a world he did not create.
Valued knowledge and experience, not knowledge that dissipates.
What concerns us in a way, appreciating and learning from.
Working with whatever happens in everyday life.
What concerns us in a way, appreciating and learning from.
Working with whatever happens in everyday life.
The life's a natural sequence, tranquil calm, fulfillment.
Between royalty and philosophers, little chance for the soul.
We are and rebel in everyday life.
What concerns us in a way, appreciating and learning from.
Working with whatever happens in everyday life.
The wise are not learned, the learned are not wise.
Matters beyond our reach smile at harmony.
That exists naturally between heaven and earth.
What concerns us in a way, appreciating and learning from.
Working with whatever happens in everyday life.

The fair crowd was awed, but a little taken aback by Chang's performance with the heavenly babies and moms. As they descended back to the ground, Lao Tsu's image ascended to the heavens, although, stopping briefly to hug Chang and Kwan Yin.

"Look, Hutely, the forest is glowing, and the sky is changing color."

"That's compliments of Tu Ti, Danny boy," Hutely barked out excitedly.

"Absolutely, Hutely, there he is! He's dancing among the trees that are blinking different earth tones as he passes them."

"He is celebrating the life of Lao Tsu and the enlightened 'Way' he shined on the world," Chang cried out with happy tears heading south. The sublime, mesmerized crowd had no idea what was going to happen next. Tu Ti abruptly stopped dancing, sensing a disturbance in the spirit realm.

Chapter 10

· · · · · · · · · · · ·

Got to Know Everything

Out of the large sandbox catapulted flaming terracotta soldiers. They wore thick coats unaffected by the flames. Their hair was up in buns that resembled wicks. They looked like charging demonic candles. Li Si and Fu Su's father sent them to destroy the last remaining remnants of the Confucian Classics and anyone that stood in their way. His immortality wish depended on it. They invaded the God of Five Roads' underworld sanctuary's time passages, charring familial chords of correspondence as they went.

Dozens of descendants were set ablaze and flung in all directions. Hot sand whipped fairgoers' faces. In all, fifty terracotta soldiers leapt out of the sandbox. They were immediately confronted by Kwan Yin's forces. Out of the expanding lotus flower slithered over a hundred colorful sparkling snakes. The viper fireman spouted water on the fairgoers and at the glowing hellish intruders. The large Asian tigers loaded up the wounded and set them in a cart attached to the master mule. Hutely had me douse the saddlebags with water supplied by one of the snakes. Chang and I boarded the burro as Tu Ti and Fu Su joined the fight. Hutely raced toward the magic ferry where Chu Yuan was waiting to immediately dunk the injured into the regenerating black water. Angels of mercy gave them fresh fruit to alleviate their tormented souls after their bodies healed.

Once her protective skin was safe, the immense Jade Dragon took flight out of the well. She swooped down on the battlefield where the sparkling snakes were having trouble keeping the flaming terracotta soldiers extinguished. The dense, concentrated, and pressurized clay

71

would simply reignite as the water evaporated. Fortunately, the fire-breathing dragon's flames were too extreme for the terracotta soldiers. Before they reignited, she blasted them with volcanic-like heat, which exposed air bubbles in their clay and caused them to explode. Fu Su and Tu Ti lured the other soldiers into long mud patches that Tu Ti summoned up from the underworld. The terracotta tormentors simply sank and their flames extinguished. The mud hardened around them within seconds, thus, sealing them up to do no more harm.

What struck me most about the flaming intruders was they all had different faces. According to Hutely, eight thousand life-sized Qin soldiers were unearthed in 1974 at Shanxi Province in Northwest China. They were created to guard Qin Shi Huang Di in the afterlife. Hutely said they were modeled after real people who served in the first emperor's military. I guess they failed at protecting their emperor's Legalist legacy. His quest for immortality went down with the fifty terracotta soldiers.

Fenhua and the recovering descendants helped terrified, but all in one piece, fairgoers relax as they made their way back toward the still smoldering sandbox. Tu Ti brought up moisture from below to cool the sand, thus, sending billows of smoke into the air. The smoke settled into a misty haze all around the fairgrounds. Through the haze at the top of the lotus flower stood a familiar figure that became clearer as the fog thinned. It was the spiritual image of Confucius. Kwan Yin bowed in respect as he spoke to the crowd.

"I praise the courage and bravery exhibited this day to preserve the Duke of Zhou's legacy," he said, bowing through the mist. The descendants were former students at the Confucian school. He demanded that they should be prepared to lay down their lives for their principles. He expected them to take up arms against tyranny fearlessly. If necessary, create a "Godly company of martyrs" on behalf of the common good.

Fenhua asked Confucius, "What can you tell us about death?"

"You don't understand life," said Confucius. "How can you understand death?" he added sternly.

"How should one serve spirits?" Fu Su asked.

"When you can adequately serve men, then you can serve spirits," Confucius answered in a more relaxed tone.

"Please talk about heaven, Master Confucius," Chang pleaded in a reverent, sincere voice. I really doubted that Confucius would answer her question. Hutely told me that Confucius seldom discussed matters about heaven. Some felt that Confucius was insincere, or even skeptical about heaven. Others even thought he might have been an atheist. To my surprise, he smiled and then addressed her question.

"I always felt that heaven was a vaguely constructed moral force in the universe," he said, gazing out at the traumatized fairgoers who had faced down deadly Legalist immorality. "It is striving individuals who do heaven's work. 'Heaven helps those who help themselves.'" Fu Su and the majority of descendants stood up and cheered. Confucius paused for a minute, but then said sorrowfully, "Many times the wicked benefit but thankfully not today. I always felt that heaven wouldn't let me fail in solving all the people's ills," said Confucius whose image began to fade. I needed just a few more words of wisdom from Confucius before his consciousness faded.

"What about living life or the afterlife, Mr. Confucius?" I asked, which elicited teeth grinding from Hutely.

"It's the qualitative not the quantitative aspect of one's life," said Confucius before disappearing into the mystic.

"Mr. Confucius, Dan?" Hutely wearily whinnied.

"Absolutely, Hutely! In late Middle English, it was an abbreviation for master."

"Okay, Mr. Dan, good show, old boy. Here is another Confucian quote to learn by," Hutely said, looking straight at me, "'don't be a recluse or simply follow the crowd.'"

"Absolutely, Hutely. That sounds like 'No man's an island and mob rule.'"

"Close enough, Danny boy. You almost nailed it, again." Before I could respond, Fu Su ascended the lotus flower, hugged Kwan Yin and, from personal experience, gave a cautionary perspective on Confucianism. He invited me to help him deliver his message in song. Both heaven and earth glowed rainbow colors compliments of Tu Ti as we sang.

Writing papers, the small group takes many steps.
Got to know everything, got to know everything.
Putting names on vital things, many words.

Planting trees beyond them, planting trees beyond them.
As busy as ants spoiling the picnic, picking up pieces dropped from heaven above, ah...
Divides abstract things, rushing back.
Not to know criminal, not to know criminal.
Seeks knowledge for heaven's sake, abstract views.
Complex rituals, complex rituals.
As busy as ants spoiling the picnic, picking up pieces dropped from heaven above, ah...
As busy as ants spoiling the picnic, picking up pieces dropped from heaven above, ah...
Writing papers, the small group takes many steps.
Got to know everything, got to know everything.
As busy as ants spoiling the picnic, picking up pieces dropped from heaven above, ah...

Once off the lotus flower, Chang rushed into Fu Su's arms. "That must have been hard for you to admit, Fu Su," Chang said, gazing into his eyes longingly.

"True Confucian reform shouldn't lead to Legalist tyranny! My father's reign of terror, though unifying, must never threaten people's happiness again. Confucius really wanted people to be happy and serve society," he concluded with a deep sigh.

"You are so right, my love. Taoist rebellions are the result of well-meaning Confucian activism. Unfortunately it falls on Taoist rebels to end imperial extremism," she said in a concerned yet sympathetic voice.

After overhearing their conversation, I couldn't help but think that there must be a better way, or at least another school of thought, to serve as a guide for the Chinese to achieve happiness.

Chapter 11

· · · · · · · · · · · ·

The Quest for Happiness Through Enlightenment

The image of Confucius settled nerves and brought the fairgoers back to their kiosks and puppet shows. Puppeteers readied their marionettes for more shows. Fenhua and his troupe put on the first play to calm the crowd and for the benefit of the books. Fenhua narrated the Confucian play that featured Confucius and a grieving mother and wife.

"A crying woman passed Confucius in the state of Lu one day. He asked her what the matter was. She told him that a tiger had devoured her father-in-law, husband, and son over the past few weeks. Confucius asked her, 'Why don't you move, woman?'

"'There is no oppressive government here, only tigers,' she answered, drying her eyes."

Fenhua looked out over the crowd and said, "Remember what Confucius says, my friends, 'oppressive government is fiercer and more feared than a tiger.'"

"Shouldn't the government have protected her family, Hutely?" I spoke out. "That might increase happiness or at least prevent sadness."

"You've got a point, Dan," Hutely whinnied, but it was Fu Su who supplied a viable answer.

"Princes, like me, in the 'Warring States Period,' being perceived as fiercer than a tiger was considered smart. A natural leader was hardworking, indifferent, and ruled harshly."

"He needs to make sure the tiger doesn't eat him," said Chang, touting Taoist sarcasm.

"Those princes should realize that we are all one, but most only see themselves and turn to cruel Legalism like many Qin princes did," Fu Su concluded.

"So you see, Danny boy, the road to happiness needs an enlightened school of thought that takes into account human suffering," said Hutely.

"Absolutely, Hutely!" I yelled, venting my frustration.

According to Hutely, the Confucian Classics were back in the books. Hutely once again pulled the cart down to the magic ferry with Chang, Fu Su, and I riding comfortably in the back. Although this time there was bedding that looked familiar. We boarded the ferry, cart and all. Chu Juan opened Hutely's saddlebags and stripped the completed pages of their protective skin covers. The massive Jade Dragon arose from the black swirling water and welcomed back her unique skin. Her whole body seemed to wriggle with joy as she flew up the newly formed well through time. Chu Juan put the completed manuscripts back in Hutely's saddlebags gently with care.

Tu Ti once again started the revolving theater which at first only showed earth-tone light values. Images began swirling around the cylindrical theater. A large beautiful palace appeared with royal servants attending to a prince's every need. There were huge courtyards that stretched hundreds of feet with large gates preventing anyone from entering or getting out for that matter. Tu Ti added narration.

"On the subcontinent of India's Eastern region, Siddhartha Gautama was pampered and shielded from all the woes of the world since childhood. By chance he ventured out into society and saw human suffering on a large scale. Gautama left his cushioned existence, which included his family, his subjects, and his privileged friends to attain enlightenment and relieve the world of its suffering."

Suddenly piano chords thundered throughout the theater with an ensemble of ringing bells, crunching leaves, and beating drums. The lyrical ball was back and bouncing rhythmically. An enlightened voice rang out with an angelic choral accompaniment to deliver Buddha's gift to the world.

The Noble Eight-Fold Path, it survives death.
Our world is setter of traps, transcendent Nirvana.
Into each one's life, Karma, ethical consequence of one's Dharma.

Illusions cause suffering, the spirit-self awakens.
The enlightened one meditates under the tree of freedom.
The enlightened one meditates under the tree of freedom.
Free of Earth's desires, no attachments.
In the inventor's land, Taoist seek Gautama.
Noble Truths contain pleasure, right views, right speech beyond measure.
To remain harmless, avoid crime, good intentions.
The enlightened one, meditates under the tree, gains wisdom.
The enlightened one, meditates under the tree, gains wisdom.

"Yes, Dan, Siddhartha Gautama is the Buddha," said Hutely, reading my mind again. "Buddhism, some say, is the dominant school of thought of China in your time, my boy."

"Absolutely, Hutely, but they may need a little Taoist agitation to fend off their president's command-economy leanings and distrust of individual rights."

"I couldn't agree more, Dan," said Chang, squeezing Fu Su's hand while flashing me a smile.

"Maybe so," Fu Su added. "However, it's time for a great purist Confucian revival," he remarked reverently as he kissed Chang's hand.

"Now, wait a cotton-picking millet! Of course, I mean minute," I said, wondering if I'd ever get that phrase right again. "Jeez," I said out of habit.

"Don't you mean Confuse?" Chang laughingly said, high-fiving Fu Su.

"Now, now, Danny boy," said Hutely, chewing on disgusting vegetation. "It's clear we need to discuss the Shakya tribe."

"Absolutely, Hutely, ah... who were they?"

"Siddhartha was born around 560 BCE and he died about 480 BCE. He was the beloved prince of the Shakya tribe. Prophecies warned his father that Gautama, instead of being a great ruler, would become an abstaining religious zealot. His old man, the king, kept him from experiencing the outside world."

"What was his father so afraid he would see, Hutely?"

"Well, Danny boy, he saw an eighty-year-old man which introduced him to the realities of aging. Another man had an ugly disease and was suffering. Finally, he saw a corpse which introduced him to the eventuality of death. As his father feared, he left his family and his accustomed luxuries."

"Absolutely, Hutely, but what did he realize?"

"He realized 'self-punishment is as destructive as self-indulgence,'" said Hutely, continuing to chew his cud. Chang then chimed in with a little cheek.

"Plain and simple, Dan, Siddhartha's royal father ignored the people's suffering and hopelessness, so Sid, out of curiosity, set out to change things starting with himself," Chang concluded, inviting a Taoist dialogue.

Chapter 12

· · · · · · · · · · · ·

Confucian Revival University

(Han Happiness)

Jia Yi answered Chang's invitation. You know, the same character that resurrected Chu Juan's lament. It was slightly after another Taoist rebellion, but he was qualified to help us fulfill our Historical Guide Academy mission. Jia Yi appeared as the revolving theater stopped, and he looked a lot like Tu Ti. They greeted one another, which touched off a dynamic light show. It was so bright, Hutely had me attach clip-on shades to his glasses. Jai Yi proceeded to have the ferry floor.

"Thank you, brother, for that colorful welcome!" he said, but then bowed to each of us repeatedly. With Hutely's approval, he then handed over the floor to Chang.

"Before the purist reinstatement of Confucianism, the Han found opportunity from disunity," she said again squeezing Fu Su's hand. Hutely threw in an approving grunt for good measure as Chang continued to speak. "Liu Bang, who called himself Gaozu, seized power from the last Qin warlord Xian Yu. He declared himself emperor in 202 BCE. Keep in mind that the Taoists were waiting in the wings. For a decade and half, things were a little more moderate, but laws were still an instrument of coercion for the ruler. After his death, his wife Lu Zhi, better known as the Empress Dowager Lu, showed her vengeful side and had his brothers killed and had his mistresses mutilated. She claimed filial piety like many in the future,

79

but Taoists weren't buying it. The people executed her and the entire Lu family. Emperor Wen then ascended to power, which paved the way for a purist Confucian revival."

"Well said, Chang," said Fu Su.

"I know," said Chang, which elicited Hutely's laughing-chainsaw reaction. He stopped when Tu Ti pointed out that a leafy treat hung near his snout. The munch was on. Tu Ti then had all of us get into the mule cart. He gave Hutely a spirited slap on his set-down, and we rolled off the magic ferry. I was amazed at how similar things looked to previous magic-ferry exits. Once past the burial grounds and heading toward the farms, Hutely stopped to pick up a small old hitchhiker and a woman who was assisting him.

"Greetings, Fu Sheng," said Hutely, "need a lift?" Fu Sheng did look a little worse for wear but not bad for a ninety-year-old. "I see you brought your daughter."

"He doesn't speak so well, but he's glad to see you," she answered with a tearful smile. "May we see his manuscripts?" she said, slightly wheezing and out of breath. At Hutely's behest, we helped Fu Sheng and his daughter into the cart. I jumped on Hutely's saddlebags and retrieved the manuscripts with the characters fully restored. He and she shed a tear when they saw the fully restored Book of Documents, Book of Odes, Book of Changes, Book of Rites, Spring and Autumn Annals, and the Tao de Ching. Jia Yi put his arm around the sobbing hero who risked his life to preserve China's future. We all got a little choked up at this point. Now it was time to hand over the documents to Han historians.

"Where are we, Hutely?" I asked as we made our way past the farmlands.

"We're in the new capital city of the Han, Changan, my boy.

"I'm a little confused, Hutely."

"Naturally, Danny boy... what about?"

"Wasn't the first Han emperor's name Kao Tsu?"

"Very good, Dan, you were paying attention in history class. Leaders were often known by different names," Hutely insisted as we entered the royal compound escorted by Han foot soldiers.

Next thing I knew, we were in the presence of the second great emperor of the Han, King Wu (140–87 BCE). His court all applauded as we entered. It was a very colorful court. Everything was red and gold, including the dress of the royals. Magicians, counselors, and clairvoyants were the emperor's advisers. They made up a sizable part of the bureaucracy along with appointed officials. Powerful families were increasingly loyal to the emperor who genuinely believed in the glory of the empire.

This emperor had a flare for pomp and ceremony. He was a learned person, and he welcomed us warmly, yet he spoke in a regal, powerful voice. We all bowed and knelt on golden pillows across from the royals and in front of the servants. He directed his remarks to Fu Sheng and his daughter.

"We are indeed honored to have you here again, Fu Sheng. You have earned the title of Master Fu for your protection and knowledge of the Confucian Shangshu, Documents, manuscript. Even though you speak in an ancient Qin dialect, your daughter has been invaluable in transcribing it into a Han dialect. Thank you, Madam Sheng, for interpreting your father's words for the benefit of all!" The crowd once again applauded.

Madam Sheng bowed in response toward the emperor, but then she bowed to her father to signify his great contribution. She then gave all the manuscripts to the court scholars who had been previously charged with reconstructing the classics. Emperor Wu had handpicked each scholar and founded an Imperial University for them to teach at. The Confucian Classics became the leading curriculum of the Han.

We all just stood there knowing that our efforts had born fruit. Hutely high-hoofed me and thanked me for once again traveling through time and making a difference for humanity. Out of the royals emerged Fenhua. We were all so glad to see him! He hugged all of us repeatedly and thanked us for our part in saving the Confucian Classics. Fenhua had us sit on our golden pillows as King Wu addressed his court again.

"Along with the successful reconstruction of the classics, this administration will not allow any suppressed doctrines. Men of humble birth showing good moral fiber, like Confucius wished, have already been appointed to my court. No matter one's stars, if they pass exams at the university, they will be welcome to serve as officials of the empire."

"Looks like Emperor Wu has things well in hand, Hutely. Everyone benefits under his rule," I said, but not fully understanding the significance of political motives.

"Quite true, Danny boy. But there is a method to his madness."

"Absolutely, Hutely, he wants to promote the people through Confucian methods."

"Depends what people you're talking about. Younger men of humble birth were more compliant and loyal, rather than the older, landed rich who sought to increase their importance. Furthermore, men selected by his examinations were supporters rather than strong-minded advisers."

"Absolutely, Hutely, so politics is politics. American nominating conventions have always bordered on the ceremonial absurd," I said as Chang and Fu Su listened to our conversation. They nodded as Hutely schooled me on the ways of the real world where craft is king.

"You see, Dan. In your time, Gipper's Gavel, false claims involving weapons of mass destruction, and voter fraud along with the influences of secret societies all contribute to disunity. But ironically, ceremony plays a key role in keeping things from spiraling out of control."

"Absolutely, Hutely, I believe Alexis de Tocqueville, who was a French aristocrat and a European minister who also wrote Democracy in America, said America's strength was in her people's binding associations, organizations, and groups."

"Yes, indeed, Dan, they all have ceremonial rituals that keep your country united. But any happy story, as you know, has conflicts. The press loves a good juicy story. They can help to join societal forces or cause them to splinter apart. China's cultural homogeneity collaborated well with a leader like the Duke of Zhou at the helm."

"I couldn't agree more," said Fenhua, "but it's time to go. Your work is done here." Fenhua escorted us out of the royal palace and hooked Hutely up to the mule cart as we all jumped in. He bade us farewell and started back toward the palace.

"Aren't you coming?" I asked.

"No, Dan, my work has just begun here," he said, bowing, and added, "I must continue the Duke of Zhou's excellent work."

I started to feel a little sad as we mule-carted it again toward the magic ferry, but it was time to travel on now that history was back on track. Going past the burial grounds made me think of all the great people who paved the way to make society a better place. I felt I was a better person having met Song, the Duke of Zhou, and all who befriended us along the way.

Qu Yuan greeted us from the ferry one last time. We floated over the rice floor and took our seats. In an instant, Tu Ti appeared as the well encapsulated us. The cylindrical theater formed and started spinning again, but this time inviting more than our eyes and ears. Suddenly Qu Yuan grabbed Jai Yi and both disappeared into the black swirling water.

"Men overboard!" I yelled hysterically. To my surprise, Fu Su, Chang, and Hutely had brooms in hoof and hand and were sweeping the rice into the water. Tu Ti paddled the water to help the rice sink to its final destination.

"They're off to write a lament and attend a Dragon Boat Festival, my boy," said Hutely who started looking a little strange.

"Okay, anything makes sense now, but where did Fu Su and Chang wander off to?"

"Two lovers each knowing the way will adopt a third school of thought to heal the consequences of rebirth, rebellion, and reincarnation," Tu Ti said, but then vanished. Upon the revolving screen shown Buddhist monks being led to a Taoist temple by Fu Su and Chang. They waved to us as the screen fizzled out. I turned to Hutely who gave me one last thought to ponder.

Chapter 13

· · · · · · · · · · · ·

Wake Up

"Out of rebellion, disunity seeks resolution to unify the thirteen who seek democracy."

"Absolutely, Samantha?" The mule cart was now my comfortable bed, and Hutely had morphed into my cocker spaniel. The revolving theater was now my flat-screen TV, and it was airing a documentary about China. Go figure, right. It was showing Xi Jinping's consolidation of power, which included the removal of Hu Jintao who had been a respected leader and proponent of economic reforms during China's most favored nation period. It showed Jiang Zemin's picture because he had just recently passed away. He had taken over for Deng Xiaoping after the Mao years. He was a driving force who led China into economic prosperity. Some called him eccentric, but he showed a joyous lust for life. He was gracious, funny, and very smart. His death was a bad omen for individual liberties in China under Xi.

That night I couldn't help but think about Hutely's last words he said to me before I woke up. Samantha gave me one of those looks that said turn off the light and go to sleep. "Okay, okay, Hutely, I mean Samantha! You win." Dozing off, I wondered how the United States managed to establish an enlightened form of government. Who were the enlightened thinkers that influenced our forefathers? What obstacles and dangers did they overcome? We avoided the dictatorship that was now seizing current world powers. If I only had a guide to show me the Enlightened Road to Democracy. I don't remember turning out the light, but fortunately another light turned on.

The End

Selected Bibliography

Creel, H. G. *Chinese Thought: From Confucius to Mao Tse-Tung.* Mentor Books, The New American Library of World Literature, 1960.

Dynamic Design Industries. *I Ching A Philosophical Prophecy.* Anaheim, California: 1972.

Fairbanks, John King. *China Old and New.* Cambridge/Massachusetts: Harvard University Press, 1976.

Hoff, Benjamin. *The Tao of Pooh.* E.P. Dutton, 1982

Meskill, John T. *An Introduction to Chinese Civilization.* Lexington, Massachusetts, Toronto: D. C. Heath and Company, 1973

Rosenberg, William G. and Marilyn B. Young. *Transforming Russia & China Revolutionary Struggle in the Twentieth Century.* New York, Oxford: Oxford University Press, 1982.

Waldherr, Kris. *The Book Of Goddesses.* Hillsboro, Oregon: Beyond Words Publishing Inc., 1996.

https://en.wikipedia.org/wiki/Fu_Sheng_(scholar)

https://en.wikipedia.org/wiki/Duke_of_Zhouhttps://en.wikipedia.org/wiki/Qu_Yuan

https://en.wikipedia.org/wiki/Rebellion_of_the_Three_Guards

https://en.wikipedia.org/wiki/Duke_of_Zhou

About the Author

Dan Tilley was born in Port Jefferson, Long Island, New York, in 1960, with a European ancestry—Irish and French. He is the cofounder of "Durango Citizens Against Forced Relocation" and "Community Happens." He and his wife, Liz, live in Albuquerque, NM. He has a BA in political science and teaches in the Albuquerque School District.